of GODS *and* DEVILS *and all* IN BETWEEN

For information contact
www.deerwoodpress.com

Book and Cover design by Lynn Harrod
Edited by William McCoy
Photos by Pexels – Pixabay

ISBN: 978-1-7367234-0-1 (ePub edition)
ISBN: 978-1-7367234-4-9 (Paperback edition)

First Edition: May 2021
Second Edition: February 2025

of

GODS

and

DEVILS

and all

IN BETWEEN

Book One

LYNN HARROD

For Bella and her creative spirit.

_____

The Lord of the Moon

Northhall Manor was one of the most breathtaking homes in the University Historic District, especially on mornings like today, with fresh snow blanketed over the picturesque town. Anyone who grew up in Salt Lake City was familiar with it. The annual Winter Solstice Celebration and Sundance Film Festival drew crowds from all over the country, and in the heart of it all stood the famed mansion. Its three stories of Federal Colonial charm – red brick and white oak trim – invited tourists to take group photos from the curb.

If Benjamin Franklin lived in Utah, Ria thought as she gazed up at the house. She stood by the old well in the front yard, a box with gold-and-silver gift wrapping in hand. The glittery bow dwarfed the box, which was the size of a paperback novel.

Ria Riveras was intimately familiar with the property. Her mentor, Professor Warren Northhall, had lived there his whole life, as did the three generations of Northhalls before him. They were teachers and administrators at Chambers University, bound to both the institution and its historic neighborhood. Ria longed for such a rich legacy.

Born in the industrial city of Modesto in Central California, Ria worked her way through college, baking pan dulce at her mother's panadería while carrying a dual major in Experimental Psychology and Behavioral Science at Sacramento State. Even she marveled at her endurance of such a workload.

Ria met Professor Northhall during her freshman year when he was the keynote speaker at a San Francisco conference on Behavioral Medicine. Ria seemed calm and pleasant when they shook hands, citing that she had only recently discovered his extensive body of work with the developmentally disabled.

She lied. Ria saw him as a rock star. If the local mall had sold posters of Professor Warren William Northhall III when she trudged through adolescence, escaping high school with an early completion certificate, those posters would have adorned her room, at least her corner of it. They'd have been thumb-tacked to the thin wood paneling walls of her tiny bedroom, above the bed she shared with two younger brothers.

Looking up at her idol's face, their hands still clasped, Ria's starstruck eyes and wide smile belied her envy. Beyond her admiration for the man's talent and work, she wanted to *be* Professor Northhall, for he'd achieved everything she wanted in life, including a tenure at Chambers and all the respect and accolades that came with it.

Ria quickly and easily impressed Northhall with her work. By the end of that weekend conference, he'd thoroughly convinced her to start a new life at Chambers University, both as a postgraduate and one of his proteges. Less than a month later, she moved seven-hundred miles from Modesto, California to Salt Lake City, Utah, to a studio apartment on Denver Street near Liberty Park. The accommodation was meager but all hers, the university within a mile. Within those hallowed halls, Professor Warren Northhall would be her sunrise and sunset over the next four years, his wisdom and guidance enriching and transforming her in ways she'd only dreamed about.

None of it could have prepared her for what lay ahead.

That snowy Sunday morning, standing by the well, she looked at the gold-and-silver gift box in her hands and hoped she made a wise choice. As she walked up the steps to the grand door, the little box felt important, perhaps more than it should have.

Ria entered Northhall Manor with a quickened pulse. The tiles under her feet, the smell of old books and mahogany and musty wool rugs, it should have all felt familiar, but that morning was different. Though she had spent countless days and nights there – usually working with research teams under tight deadlines – that morning gave her an odd, unnerving, fresh perspective, as if taking in the historic home's grandeur for the first time. When she first arrived years before, she presented herself as an antisocial tangle of nerves. She stood in awe and excitement and doubt, but soon came to regard the mansion as a second home. Though she couldn't explain it, a somber veil fell upon her as she passed its threshold now, joining the festive, well-dressed crowd.

Ria had dismissed her usual pink sweats, floral sweater, and rain boots, choosing instead to endure an elegant formal dress, just as the sealed invitation required. Her puffy pink knit cap stayed home as her long, wavy brown hair sat exposed, ribboned in a tidy bun. She denied herself her daily Americana with extra cream and sugar – plus a second one with Splenda for the professor – for that morning's affair called for more frilly offerings. Champagne and strawberries and eclairs sat in lovely rows to go with the speeches and farewell toasts, one after another, all in an outpouring of love for the professor.

Ria knew he must have had a monumental announcement to make. He rarely invited people to his famous home and always limited his proteges to the kitchen, parlor, and library. To have dozens of faculty and students in the grand foyer gathered at the base of the stairs, champagne flutes raised, dressed in their Sunday best, felt like a memorial service.

How true her instincts would prove to be.

"Ladies and gentlemen," Professor Northhall said from the top of the stairs, arms outstretched, "my many friends and colleagues." His warm, weathered voice echoed through the old house. He rubbed his thick salt-and-pepper beard in thought, a "tell" that betrayed his true feelings to Ria.

He's nervous, she thought.

"Thank you all for coming on this chilly, drizzly morning. Most of your hairdos have withstood the dismal climate." The group laughed as the professor worked the room like a showman. "At least you still have enough beautiful hair to fret over. Lord, how I miss that burden." The crowd laughed again as he slide his hand across his thinning scalp. The Professor rarely told jokes, but when he did, they were always self-depreciating.

He's scared?

He's never scared.

"All laughter aside," Northhall said, "allow me to find my way to the point. Some of you have been privy to wildly running rumors about me." He nodded at the room's sudden silence. "Maybe you've heard that I'm transferring to another school, or being fired for openly mocking the dean for his extreme political views. I wish it were the latter. The look on Edgar's face alone would be worth the termination." The group laughed again. Some applauded the absurd notion.

Ria stood in the middle of the crowd, clutching her gold-and-silver gift box. She stood out for several reasons. Though she certainly earned her place there, she never shook the feeling that she didn't quite belong. Perhaps it was the fact that she was a young Mexican girl from a working-class Catholic family holding court with well-to-do White, middle-aged Mormons. It was certainly something to ponder. At least Northhall was a simple, non-practicing Christian.

"Many of you may have surmised, despite the ridiculous speculation, that our gathering today on this lovely, snowy morning is a going-away party. I'm here to tell you... you're correct."

The group was visibly aghast, which wounded Northhall. He felt he was abandoning them. "I could never keep a secret from this group. That's what happens when one surrounds himself with brilliant minds. Sadly, the rumors are true. You're all here today to bid this old man farewell."

There were no hushed murmurs, no quiet questions, no exchanged glances. The group was still and silent, awaiting the professor's next word, hoping that one dark rumor wasn't true.

"I'm dying, my friends," Northhall said, matter-of-fact, finding it difficult to look at the shocked and sad faces before him. "Colorectal cancer. Are there two more vile, obscene words to share with loved ones? I submit there are not. If my doctor is to be believed, plus the second and third opinions she sought, I'll likely leave this world and all its glories within a year."

Having spent many hours each day with her mentor, seeing his health deteriorate with every cough and stumble, the news did not surprise Ria, yet her stomach twisted upon hearing confirmation of her fears. The man whom she admired from the time she first realized her life's calling, the man she came to see as the surrogate grandfather and best friend she relied on for so many years, would soon vanish from her life. His departure would steal a piece of her soul.

"With my clock winding down, I'm taking an early retirement from Chambers University to follow other pursuits, to hopefully tie them neatly with a bow for the next generation of scholars to study. You all know that I have contract work elsewhere, work that has meant a great dealt to me over thirty-plus years. It calls to me now. I'm leaving our hallowed classrooms to my capable colleagues so that I may chase my passions while there's still breath in my body. I hope you understand."

Northhall pulled a silver pocket watch from his coat and checked the time. He raised his glass and spoke to the anxious crowd but looked directly at Ria, pleasantly surprised to see her.

"Always remember the time we had shared. The Lord grants no greater gift."

By the early afternoon, most of the well-wishers had gone. After an hour of corner conversations over wine and cheese and pastry, their last opportunity to bid the professor a fond adieu came and went. The grand house was now mostly silent, with only a handful of confidants still lingering in its historic halls, hanging on Northhall's many anecdotes and retrospectives.

Ria downed her champagne and roamed the estate. As she felt when she first arrived that morning, she saw the manor in a new light, as if it were both the first and last time she'd ever set foot in the famous house. In particular, Ria saw the manor for the rooms the professor had forbidden her to enter, most notably the secret room that she'd discovered six months prior, and the unusual manner in which to access it. Today would be her last chance to quell her curiosity.

Looking around the parlor to ensure that no one was watching, Ria placed her paperback-sized gold-and-silver gift box on a fireplace mantle and walked into the next room, the professor's famous library. The haven of knowledge proved so awe-inspiring that *Time Magazine* wrote a featured article about it. Even if it had been empty, the elegant room adorned with wooden Art Deco accents and copper inlays, all designed by celebrated architect Frank Lloyd Wright, was its own historic masterpiece.

Ria Riveras herself featured in the magazine as well – four issues back – for her unique life story of hard work prevailing over socioeconomic limitations. She always treasured that article.

Stepping alone into the incredible, book-lined room, she approached a wall-length bookshelf dense with texts from a lifetime of study. She walked to a section of the bookshelf tucked in a corner, a section whose slightly discolored wood contrasted with the rest of the collection. Ensuring no witness, she placed her hand along the spine of a book on native Bolivian birds.

She pulled the book out a few inches and promptly lifted a poster of Ivan Pavlov from the wall to the right. Behind the poster was a simple red button, now brightly lit, embedded in the wainscoting. She'd discovered the button and how to access it many months before, but refrained from exploring it out of respect for Professor Northhall's privacy. Given that he was not long for this world, she saw the moment as her last chance to see the true passion of her mentor's life's work.

With a press of the button, the wainscoting slid aside, revealing the hidden study she long suspected of hiding in plain sight all these years.

Ria entered the secret room.

The study stretched before her. A long, narrow room, its walls were plastered with aerial maps, line charts, and black-and-white photographs of people she'd never met and buildings she'd never seen. The sight was overwhelming. Three waste paper baskets overflowing with crumpled papers and two drafting tables cluttered with takeout food boxes told Ria that her mentor had spent many long nights tucked away in there.

She turned to close the door but kept it ajar. The obscure manner of entering this room had taken months of observation. If the bookcase had shut and locked behind her, getting out might have been another puzzle.

The oversized wall maps were the first items to catch her eye. Some displayed the Greater Salt Lake County area while others detailed a remote region called "Uyuni." It sounded familiar. Japanese forest? Native American ruins? Small mountain town in Russia? Any of these guesses were reasonable, for Northhall was a world traveler, flying to distant locales each month. The world's many cultures and languages fascinated him. If not for the allure of psychology, he'd surely have been a brilliant anthropologist.

One map was a blown-up satellite photo of what appeared to be a desert at the western base of the Andean continental mountain range in South America. A single red thumbtack within a circle marked the middle of the expanse, doubling as the period to a large question mark written with a red felt pen.

There were other thumbtacks protruding from other maps, with yarn connecting them in an intricate web, all leading back to that question mark, back to the vast desert in Uyuni.

Ria grabbed a compass from a drafting table and traced the circle at the question mark, measuring the diameter of the unknown location.

"Two-fifths kilometer," she whispered, "a hair less than half a mile."

"A hair more than a quarter-mile," Professor Northhall said from the open doorway in his soft, grizzled voice, piercing the silence. "That old compass doesn't hold a candle to a military satellite photo array." He checked the time on his pocket watch.

Ria scooted from the map wall as if denying the fact that she was scrutinizing his work. "I'm sorry, Professor. The door was open."

"Was it?" Professor Northhall looked at his disciple in awe. He stood paralyzed by his prized protege's intuition, intelligence, and determination.

"The door was already open and I..."

"No, my dear," Northhall said. "I've got security cameras that show otherwise. There are four that you can clearly see from the library and two more that no one sees. You've never lied to me before. Why start now?"

Ria abandoned any notion of deceiving the professor. It would be like trying to fool Sherlock Holmes armed himself with modern surveillance methods.

"Be honest with me, Ria. How did you gain entry into my study? There's no use concerning yourself over whether I'd be angry with you. I'll be dead by month's end and therefore unable to exact malicious revenge."

"Month?" Ria asked, concerned. "I thought the doctors gave you a year."

"That's what I told my loving entourage. No need to plunge them into sorrow so soon. Four, maybe five weeks, is my doctors' best collective guess. At least we get to enjoy one final White Christmas together."

"So, I'm not fired?" Ria asked, confused.

"That depends on your next words. I ask again, how did you gain entry?"

Ria took one more look around the fascinating study, as if it were her last opportunity. Indeed, it was, but not for the reasons she assumed. "About a year ago, I hung a photo on the wall. You and I were performing at a charity benefit."

"Sugar House Boys and Girls Club," Professor Northhall said, remembering the day fondly. "Fairmont Park. The children never saw cellos in concert before. It was quite a departure from their Top 40 pop bubble gum musings."

Ria had trouble recalling their cello duet, but continued regardless. "I noticed a seam in the wall, traced it until I realized there was a hidden door, a hidden room. These old Federal Colonial mansions often have them."

"The manor is no exception. This room was once a speakeasy." He smiled at seeing the surprise on his protege's face. "This town has always celebrated Northhall men, but certainly not for being teetotalers! Even dedicated scholars occasionally need a good stiff drink to dispel the fog and cobwebs from the brain. I've been known to entertain a Green Fairy or Dirty Martini on occasion."

"I can relate," she sighed.

"So you discovered the door, but how did you come to open it?"

"My curiosity got the better of me. I watched you access the room several times."

She accessed my security cameras, he realized. *Bravo, Ria Riveras.*

"I assumed Dean Edgar would let me go once you passed on," she continued. "I figured today would be my last chance to see inside your mind, your 'passion' project. My apologies for violating your privacy, Professor."

"Nonsense," he said with a grin. "You're my best and brightest, Ria. I knew you'd eventually stumble your way in here. To be honest, I expected you. I just didn't know what day I'd find you here. My only surprise is how long it took you to gather the courage to take your first steps across the threshold."

"I suppose we know each other's secrets now."

"Not quite." He found it difficult to speak the words. "You've seen the inside of this room, but you haven't truly seen my 'passion' project, as you call it."

Professor Northhall confessed that he'd admired her for years. Of his five hand-picked, vetted proteges, all eager to work with him on his mysterious pursuits beyond the university and the City of Salt Lake, he always considered her the clear leader among the candidates. His hidden cameras revealed that two of them stole valuable antiques from the house, while another two hosted unbridled parties in the conservatory while he was away on business. What he saw in Ria was a loyal, studious, kind, and generous soul, even without witness.

For thirty years, the professor concealed the red button that opened the wainscoting behind a wooden award plaque bolted solidly to the wall. He replaced it with a simple poster of Ivan Pavlov to observe who would see past his subterfuge and accept his invitation to enter.

Satisfied with his assessment of her, he revealed the truth.

"I want to be honest with you, Ria. The reason I'm retiring early from Chambers University is not because I'm retiring early from life. I'm not actually dying."

The usually straightforward and logical professor sounded cryptic, something Ria was unaccustomed to.

"You don't have terminal cancer?" she asked.

"Oh, I do have cancer, and it is most assuredly terminal," he said, finding it difficult to explain. In no way did he want her to think he'd become senile, like the Northhall men who preceded him. "But I can prolong its process, extend my old age, and continue my life's work. It involves the Question Mark on the map, that quarter-mile area in the Uyuni Salt Flats of Bolivia. It's what I want to share with you now."

"You can live longer in Bolivia?" Ria asked, still confused. "What exactly are you sharing with me?"

"You waited a year to learn about this mystery room. You passed my little morality test and finally found a way in, only to discover a second mystery room on the other side of the world, marked on a map. The question isn't, 'What am I sharing?' The question is, 'Are you ready to open another door?'"

Ria took a moment to absorb everything her mentor was proposing.

"Here in Salt Lake?" she asked.

"Heavens, no."

"How long would I need to be away?"

Professor Northhall sighed. "My dear, did Dian Fossey ask, 'How long am I going to be out here with these damn gorillas?' Did Marie Curie ask, 'How long must I remain in this forsaken lab?' Did Edmund Hillary wonder how much longer until he reached the summit of that infernal mountain atop the Earth?"

Ria scoffed at being compared to such great minds, but she knew Northhall detested hyperbole and paused when she read his stone-serious expression. "It's that big, Professor?"

"Bigger."

"You make it sound life-changing."

"It's beyond life-changing," Northhall said, "for it will change how you see this world. I wouldn't ask you to join me if it didn't."

He knew his protege well. Such as opportunity offered everything she'd always dreamed of. Her many years of hard work, studying, research, personal sacrifice, it was all in preparation of what she called "The Big Moment."

Since she was a child, Ria wished she could feel the euphoria that swept over Howard Carter as he knelt on the sand in the Valley of Kings and first peered through a tiny hole into the inner chamber of Tutankhamen's tomb, or the mix of fear and exhilaration that the crew of the Santa Maria experienced when the eastern shore of the New World first appeared on the Atlantic horizon. She always assumed that her personal Big Moment had been the day Northhall asked her to move to Salt Lake to work under his wing. Yet, there she now stood as her mentor presented another challenge, a chance at exploring something greater.

She envisioned her future, pictured the private downtown practice she'd long sought, the clients and money and respect she deserved. She always had a clear path ahead, but now considered straying from her carefully laid plans, entrusting her detour into the wild to the eminent Professor Warren Northhall, to the paramount unknown that he wanted to unveil and unravel with her.

Bolivia.

They speak Aymaran Spanish there.

It was a dialect she used to speak with her Abuelita Nina, whose parents came from Peru's capital.

"My family is originally from Lima," she said. "Of course, you factored that in."

"Of course, I did," he said with a grin. "The Question Mark on that map is about a day's drive south from Lima. The door awaits you, my dear. It awaits us both, and I believe you are the key. You can stay here and enjoy a life of comfort at Chambers, with fond, distant memories of this old man, or you can join me for the rest of my journey where you will either share in my triumph or witness my failure."

It was too much to think about, too sudden and too quick, but her pulse raced with her mounting curiosity. "What's the next step?" she said, throwing all caution aside.

Professor Northhall smiled widely, his excitement covering his unease and fear. He checked the time on his pocket watch. "We must leave for Bolivia tonight."

* * *

After a twenty-two-hour flight with stops in Los Angeles and Lima, Ria and the professor disembarked at La Serena Airport in Chile, an airport terminal not much bigger than Northhall Manor. A young man in a white button-up shirt and denim shorts greeted them. Ria's layers of thermals, hooded sweatshirt, scarf, and khakis stood out in the contrasting dry heat.

Professor Northhall introduced him as Mateo Galvez, and he stood speechless upon meeting her. Northhall further revealed that Mateo had been the professor's guide and confidant in South America for the past fifteen years. Ria assumed Mateo worked simply as hired help, perhaps because she hadn't yet realized the immense scope of Northhall's project. It surprised her to learn that Mateo served as a respected anthropologist and yet another of the old man's proteges, whose field of study was Behavioral Science. It also startled her to observe the close relationship the two men shared. Rarely was Northhall so relaxed and talkative with someone other than a Chambers student.

Northhall had yet to provide details of his ongoing passion project, but whatever it was, Mateo had clearly played a part for the entire fifteen years in his employ.

"Are you now going to tell me where we're going?" Ria asked as they gathered their baggage. It startled Mateo to realize how little she knew.

"I want you to see it for yourself," Northhall said, almost teasing. "The answers will come, hopefully from you."

"I don't understand."

"Neither will I, not fully, until you do."

The night fell humid and silent as they piled into a pale green 1972 Land Rover Series III, an iconic utilitarian vehicle that Ria had always envisioned driving while exploring the mysteries of the world. She'd always romanticized that legendary machine, and there it waited, chosen not for its legacy but because a fifty-year-old decommissioned scout vehicle was the best they could acquire at such short notice.

The lights of the Chilean coastal civilization faded into the distance as they traveled east toward the Andean foothills. Soon, the Land Rover left behind paved roads and rumbled onto rocky terrain on a trail that seemed easy to lose sight of. Fortunately, Mateo seemed to know the route intimately. Ria sensed he could easily navigate the land even in the darkest of night.

"We should arrive by dawn," Professor Northhall told her from the front passenger seat. "If you want to take a nap, now would be a good time. I'll need your full faculties when we arrive."

The idea of sleeping as they stitched through the countryside on their way to the Question Mark was laughable. Her anticipation, coupled with the bumpy ride, kept her wide-eyed and alert. She couldn't sleep now, even if they drugged her. In contrast, Northhall reclined in his seat and slid his canvas Panama hat over his face. This path felt well worn for him, rocking him to sleep.

With her mentor knocked out for the time being, she leaned forward to speak with Mateo. "The Professor hasn't told me much," she said.

"What has he told you?" Mateo asked.

"There's a site in the Uyuni Salt Flats he's visited monthly for thirty years, where a staff of locals helps him with his research. I assume you're one of his residents."

"You could say that," Mateo replied. "Of course, I've had little luck in getting through, but from what I hear, you'll fare far better."

"Where do the funds come from?"

"That's a question for Warren. I try to stay out of anything with a dollar sign."

He calls the professor "Warren."

No one calls him that.

"What I can tell you is that we're funded well into the next century," Mateo added.

"Does everyone else on the team speak English?"

"Everyone at the house, yes."

In her mind, Ria replayed everything he said, something she often did when she was trying to figure out a situation.

He's had little luck getting through?

At the house?

"I wouldn't worry," he assured her. "You speak Spanish, yes?"

"Latin American Spanish. I also speak some Peninsular Spanish and some Portuguese if needed."

"That's good to know, but you won't need it much. Do you speak German?"

"German? No. Why would I need that?"

"It could come in handy." Mateo gripped the wheel as he plowed through a field of Cortaderia, tall grass with white plumes that almost glowed in the dark. Bounding over a rise, the field resembled a sea of feathers bowing in the breeze, a sight to behold.

The swaying masses of the Cortaderia hypnotized Ria, and she was finally succumbing to nearly two days without sleep. Her companion noticed.

"Rest now," Mateo said. "When you wake, we'll be close to the professor's house."

* * *

Ria's eyes fluttered open as the sun rose over the plains. Her back ached from sleeping on the collapsed cushion of her fifty-year-old rear bucket seat. She may as well have slept on bare metal.

In the front seat, Professor Northhall now had the wheel. Mateo sat beside him eating a sandwich. Upon seeing Ria rising forward, he handed her a bottle of water and another of his sandwiches, a simple wheat bun with roast beef and mantecoso, a pale yellow cheese, shoved inside. She recognized it from her childhood as a "Barros Jarpa," a Sunday morning treat her Abuelita Nina used to make after church. She'd since made the sandwich for herself many times, and it now comforted her to eat something from her childhood.

Biting into the sandwich, Ria sat upright and looked around, startled to see nothing but perfectly flat, white plains as far as she could see. No Cortaderia, trees, no rocks, no roads or buildings. Were it not for the clear blue sky, it looked and felt like they were traveling across the moon.

"We're finally at the salt flats," she observed.

"Finally?" Northhall said with a laugh. He pulled out his pocket watch to check the time. "We've been on them for five hours now."

"Are we nearly there? Or are we driving to the end of the Earth?"

"We're about ten minutes from the security perimeter," Mateo explained, as if that was a perfectly normal thing to say.

Ria had an overwhelming stack of questions, but kept to herself and her sandwich, keeping an eye open for anything other than salt flat plains.

Twelve minutes later, a wire fence appeared on the horizon, stretching out for miles as if wrapping around the world. They approached a tall gate guarded by two men in military gear. She didn't see any designations on their uniforms that revealed what country or military branch they served. They simply wore full-body camouflage outfitted with machetes, pistols, and rifles.

What has the professor gotten me into?

"Hola, Miguel," Northhall said to one of the approaching soldiers as he came to a stop at the gate. "Es bueno verte."

"Buenos días, Warren," Miguel replied. "Trajiste a alguien nueva. Nunca tienes invitadas."

"Ella no es una invitada," Northhall said. "Ella es parte de nuestro equipo. Se puede confiar en ella."

They called him Warren, too.

Not "Señor Northhall."

As before, Ria carefully replayed their words in her mind to analyze each utterance.

"Good morning, Miguel. It's good to see you... Good morning, Warren. You brought someone new. You never bring guests... She's not a guest. She's part of our team. We can trust her."

That's what's important out here on the moon, hundreds of miles from anything, behind fences and armed mercenaries.

We can trust her.

The guards slid the gate open, allowing them to continue miles deeper into the salt flats.

"Which military are they from?" Ria asked. "Bolivian? Peruvian? Chilean?"

"Mine," Professor Northhall said. "Private contractors. Miguel and Luis are good men."

"They're armed to the teeth," Ria noted. "What's the danger way out here? We're in the middle of nowhere. Who are they keeping out?"

"I suppose they keep people out," Northhall said. "But their job is to keep people in."

Ria considered her mentor's ominous words, but remained silent in the backseat as they rumbled onward. Moments later, as she thought of more questions, the Land Rover finally arrived at its unusual destination.

Sitting in the middle of the salt flats, surrounded by a vast nothing for hundreds of miles in all directions, was "the house."

It wasn't just any house.

It was Northhall Manor.

A stark contrast to the surrounding white plains that stretched to the horizon, the impressive structure was an exact duplicate of the historic Federal Colonial mansion in Salt Lake City, Utah, down to the trees and foliage. It was a startling, almost frightening sight.

She saw the rusty mailbox that never received mail, standing slightly crooked as she'd remembered. A municipal trash can sat at the edge of the property waiting for a Salt Lake County garbage truck that would never come. A majestic red maple tree had quaint, homemade English Tudor birdhouses, all crafted and installed by the professor's late wife, Elena. The wrens, swallows, and sandpipers of Northern Utah could never visit the lovely, tiny homes. The only detail missing was Christmas snow. Maybe it had been there, long melted and evaporated by the desert heat.

Ria knew she was seeing the impossible. The dead ground wouldn't permit the growth of White Firs, junipers, or poplars. There simply couldn't be a quaint herb garden growing aside a two-hundred-year-old settler's well. Yet there the well stood, encompassed by a semi-circular driveway for cars that didn't exist, that couldn't exist, not out here.

"What the hell am I seeing?" Ria muttered in shock, still not sure if she was awake or dreaming. "Where are we, professor?"

"We're at my ancestral home," Professor Northhall said as he parked the Land Rover in the driveway. "Rather, a perfect duplicate of it."

"You didn't just build a second house way out here," she said. "You couldn't. I mean, the minute details... all the little... I can't imagine the logistics..."

"Let's go inside," Northhall said, shutting off the Rover's engine. He looked at the late-afternoon sun and checked the time again on his pocket watch. "It'll all be clear soon."

The three of them stepped out of the vehicle into the eerie silence of the perfect facsimile she was so familiar with. She turned around and looked past the well, past the rows of Ponderosa pines that lined the driveway, expecting to see the science building of Chambers University. Instead, there was nothing but salt flats. It felt unnerving, as if someone had erased the rest of the world like sketches on a page.

Mateo looked at her with a trace of pity. He could feel her palpable, overwhelming confusion.

He'd also felt it once, long ago.

With Professor Northhall leading the way, the three scholars entered the mansion.

* * *

"I think I figured it out," Ria said as she entered the house, its interior just as perfectly detailed as its exterior. "Your project involves terraforming, right? Growing vegetation in lifeless dirt, creating thriving, livable habitats in the most remote, desolate places. Climate control?"

"Not quite," Northhall said.

Ria was about to continue with her desperate theory when she saw something glittering across the room, something that simply couldn't be.

In the parlor just off the entry hall, she saw a gold-and-silver gift-wrapped box, the size of a paperback novel. Atop the fireplace mantle outside Professor Northhall's library, it sat unopened, pristine.

It was her gold-and-silver box, her farewell gift for the professor.

It was the gift she placed there, back in Salt Lake City two days before, moments before infiltrating the professor's hidden room. It seemed impossible, yet there it was, the same box, sitting in the same spot.

Northhall saw his protege's mind breaking apart. "We obviously need to talk. Now is as good as time as any..."

"Warren, you've come early," said an elderly woman as she entered the parlor, her Spanish accent underneath perfect English. She wore a sundress whose colors matched the ribbons in her long, braided, silver hair.

"Donnamaria is the caretaker of this estate," the professor said. He turned to her, his face uncertain. "I see he's got you in that dress again."

"I don't mind. It's comfortable." Donnamaria couldn't help but stare in awe at the fresh-faced new member of their team.

Following behind her was a tall, middle-aged Caucasian man, light brown hair perfectly coiffed, his white Polo shirt and jeans fitted to his lean frame.

Professor Northhall introduced the two caretakers as Donnamaria Solíz and Troy Walker, respectively, two trustees of his "second home." They seemed warm and friendly, eager to greet someone new.

"At last we meet!" Troy said in a heavy southern drawl. "Gabriel's been waiting for you. He's in the conservatory."

"We haven't briefed her yet," Northhall quickly said, silencing his comrades.

"Who's Gabriel?" Ria asked. "Are you going to 'brief' me before I met him, whoever he is?"

"My dear," Northhall said, suddenly finding it difficult to face her. "No doubt you have many theories and questions about where we are and how this house can exist. You're right in concluding that I couldn't have possibly built this place, and you're right in assuming that our benefactor must surely pour a fortune into our project. But the mystery is not the place, rather the person in the next room."

"Gabriel."

The Question Mark.

"I want you to know that everything I said about you is true," Northhall said. "I do so admire you, and I've always considered you my best and brightest. But the truth is, I chose you because he asked for you. Please keep an open mind."

He asked for me?

Professor Northhall gestured for Mateo and Troy to open a set of French doors beyond the staircase. Northhall and his three trustees remained at the entry, waiting for Ria to enter.

"The door is open," Northhall said, repeating his familiar, ominous words. "Time to move forward. I'll be with you."

"We all will," Mateo added, trying not to appear nervous.

Ria's instincts forbade her from taking another step, but she'd come so far, not just in the past few days but across her entire life.

Northhall's team also seemed apprehensive, slightly afraid, but offered smiles and nods of encouragement. Ria nodded back.

Together, the group entered the conservatory.

None of them knew what would happen next.

* * *

Lynn Harrod

This Northhall Manor's conservatory was a massive greenhouse abundant with life. English ivy, Star jasmine, and Kentucky wisteria climbed up the glass walls, framing a breathtaking view of the property's impossibly exquisite garden. White decorative wrought-iron tables and chairs – enough for a party of two-hundred – sat on salmon clay patio bricks arranged in a cross-hatch pattern like fine wood inlay flooring. The scent of the permanently blooming flora permeated the air like a heavenly perfume.

Walking through the familiar doors felt surreal, into the one area of the house strikingly heightened from its Utah counterpart. In the middle of the grand room, staring out at a pond in the garden, stood a young man in a blue three-piece suit. He held a magazine at his side. Diana, Princess of Wales, smiled on the cover, the contentious headline beneath: "What is The Queen keeping from Diana?"

Sensing company, the well-dressed man greeted everyone without taking his eyes off the garden.

"Guten tag," he said in perfect German. "Du hast das Mädchen mitgebracht. Ich hoffe sie bleibt länger als der Junge."

"Your German is coming along well," Northhall replied. "Not as fast as you took to Russian or French, but faster than your mastery of Japanese. For now, let's return to English, shall we?"

The man in the blue suit turned and looked at Ria, his thin, black hair sitting atop a friendly, round, pale face.

"Ria Riveras," he said in a whispery voice. "You finally made it."

"Hard to believe," she said, not knowing what else to say to the mysterious man.

"I'm Gabriel." He remained at the window and extended his hand, prompting Ria to approach him to take it in a handshake. Northhall and his team remained at the French doors, breath held, allowing them the private moment.

"You know me?" Ria asked.

"Absolutely. I know all about you. I used to eat your pan dulce growing up, fresh every morning."

"You lived in Modesto?"

"No," Gabriel said, confused.

"You lived in Salt Lake?" Ria asked, searching for answers. Perhaps her mother shipped goods across state lines, unbeknownst to her.

"I was in Salt Lake for a time. I moved here when I was six."

"How long ago was that?"

"It's been a while," he smiled. "Twenty-nine years, three months, four days, six hours, nineteen minutes."

Ria quickly did the math. Nothing added up. Ria was only twenty-five years old. Her mother's panadería had only been open for eighteen years.

"You sure you ate pan dulce from our shop?" she asked.

"I'm eating one right now." Gabriel smiled as he held up an empanada de calabaza, a pumpkin-filled, baked turnover, her mother's signature pastry during the fall and winter holidays.

Ria felt sure he wasn't holding the empanada a moment ago, but perhaps she'd simply missed it. She struggled to think of something else to say. "I feel a bit underdressed," she said, nodding to his suit.

"Maybe it's me," he said. "To be honest, I wasn't sure how to dress. Perhaps the suit is too much." Gabriel raised his hand, raised two fingers. Instantly, his coat, vest, and tie vanished, leaving only his slacks and dress shirt.

Ria felt like her head was about to explode.

Mateo quickly intervened. He knew what she was going through. "Those Barros we ate in the car are long gone," he told the group. "I think we could all use something to eat."

Donnamaria took Mateo's cue. "Gabriel, let them give her a tour of the grounds while I make us something," she said. "How about cinnamon coffee cake, spring rolls, BLTs with avocado, and peach iced tea? I can have it ready in thirty minutes." They were among Gabriel's favorite foods.

"I can have it ready now," Gabriel said, raising two fingers.

"She's traveled a long way," Northhall said quickly. "We can talk over a meal later."

"But it's almost sunset."

Northhall checked his pocket watch. He turned to Ria and saw the lost look on her face. She was simply not ready to engage with Gabriel, and there was no telling what would happen if they took that chance. No guest had ever come this far. She needed to know everything first.

"Thirty minutes, Gabriel," Northhall insisted. "Please. It'll give Ria time to settle in, plus food always tastes better when Donnamaria makes it. You've always told me that."

Everyone waited in silence as Gabriel thought for a moment. "Well, I suppose if we don't have time today, we can always start over again tomorrow." He smiled and turned to the professor. "You always know best, Dad."

Dad?

"Don't let that pastry ruin your appetite," Troy said with a laugh. "Save room for those spring rolls."

"You're right, Troy," Gabriel agreed. "I can always eat it later."

The empanada de calabaza disappeared from Gabriel's hand. This time, Ria knew it wasn't her imagination. She nearly fainted from the sight of it fading away.

"Come now, Ria," Professor Northhall said, ushering her out of the conservatory. "Let us show you the garden."

As Northhall's team left, Gabriel sat in one of the wrought-iron chairs and opened the magazine in his hand.

Ria, Mateo, and the professor entered the garden. Like the rest of the property, the lush landscaping extended a few hundred yards from the house. From there, the salt flats took over, stretching to the horizon where the orange-yellow sun hovered just above. Ria was at a loss for words. She waited for someone to tell her what the hell was going on.

"I wanted you to meet him with no advanced knowledge," Northhall said. "It was important that he meet you – the real you – with none of the pretense we show him."

"What pretense?" Ria asked.

"But sitting and talking with him, having his complete attention, that's a different story. As it may happen, you need to prepare."

"You're scaring me, Professor," she said. "I've never known you to walk on eggshells around anyone. You're acting as if he's the lord of the manor and we're all his servants."

"In a manner of speaking, that's precisely the situation."

"Are you going to 'brief' me now?" she demanded, growing more agitated.

"Of course. Where to begin?"

"From the beginning! There's his childhood in Salt Lake, the days he ate my mother's food years before it was possible. Explain the vanishing suit and the empanada that materialized in his hand. You can start with why he summoned me here."

For the first time, Northhall was unsure how to proceed, as if about to break devastating news. He looked to Mateo for solace or advice, but his assistant had none.

"Alright," Northhall relented. "If I'm going back to the beginning, it'll be long before the suit or the pastry. Please keep an open mind."

* * *

Thirty-five years ago in Salt Lake City, Professor Northhall came home from the university after conducting a seminar on Contemporary Cultural Sociology. He drove in the afternoon rain, parked in his semi-circular driveway, and heard a strange noise when his engine shut off.

Within the pattering of rain, a baby whimpered. Northhall followed the sound to a spot near the well where he discovered a bassinet. A baby boy lay bundled inside, partially sheltered from the rain under the well's eave. Northhall's first impulse was to call the authorities to report that someone had abandoned an infant on his property.

Carrying the baby into his dark house, he felt a note under the blankets. The message, which had been hurriedly written on a scrap of paper, promptly changed Northhall's mind and ultimately the course of his life...

> *Gabriel is a special child who needs a special parent, one who can come to understand his needs. For your safety and the safety of others, please don't surrender him to child services. I beg you to care for him as your own, as I couldn't. I beg you to shelter him from the world. If anyone can understand and develop his mind, it must be you, Professor. But if you aren't the man I believe you to be, then no one is, and I would beg you to kill him, for I lack the courage.*
>
> *Forever in your debt,*
> *Mary*

Professor Northhall assumed he was reading the words of madness until he felt an intense heat from across the room. The dark parlor now glowed as the dormant fireplace roared to life, bursting with flame. The baby had been gazing at it from the moment they entered. Cold and damp from being out in the rain, he wanted to sit by the fire.

In their shared silence, Northhall knew what little Gabriel wanted.

The baby told him.

Northhall tenderly placed Gabriel on the rug in front of the fireplace. Now he wanted something sweet to drink.

The baby told him.

Elena Northhall came downstairs to greet her husband, surprised by what she saw, astonished by what she felt.

Over the next hour, the Northhalls discussed their next paramount decision. Despite the strange occurrences and the unexplainable connection they had with the child, the logical choice was to surrender him. For a time, that was their intention, but doctors had proclaimed that Elena could never conceive, and Fate brought a healthy baby boy to their home. Whether it was her maternal intuition, her dream realized, or the baby's inexplicable influence on them, their family union felt right.

Elena held up the note from the bassinet, pointing out that Mary, that poor, desperate woman, hadn't merely abandoned her baby at a hospital or fire station. She'd hoped that Professor Warren Northhall would care for him. It was her belief that only he could raise such a "special" boy.

The Northhalls cemented their decision to raise Gabriel over the following weeks when the infant crawled about the manor, transforming the rooms as he saw fit. With his undeveloped mind, the changes were often startling. Toys appeared on the floor. A puppy trotted forward from the shadows. Walls changed colors and patterns daily.

Most disturbingly, a young woman materialized before them and held Baby Gabriel, singing him a lullaby in the conservatory.

It was Mary.

The woman didn't acknowledge the Northhalls as she rocked the boy in her arms, for she wasn't really there. She was but a memory made flesh, willed briefly into being by Gabriel's emotional needs. She existed just long enough to put her child to sleep and write a note – the same note Northhall found in the bassinet – tucking it under the baby's blankets.

The brief, tender moment was Gabriel's memory, his last time with his mother.

As he drifted to sleep with the sun setting behind the mountains, his mother faded from sight, leaving only the little baby, bundled and alone. She only appeared in the Northhall home four more times before the infant completely forgot her.

The next six years proved difficult for the Northhalls. The professor decided early on that their adopted son would require homeschooling. Having two teachers as parents, it seemed to make sense. They would educate him, teach him right from wrong, enrich him with the different cultures of the world, all while keeping his special condition secret within the walls of Northhall Manor. They sought to hone it, control it.

For the safety of others.

Elena resigned from teaching to care for her son full time while the professor searched for a means to raise him without incident, for there were many incidents, even in his strictly sheltered life.

Defying his parents, Gabriel continued to make things appear, things that he saw on television or in a book. With a mere thought, new pets would roam the halls, comic books covered every inch of the floors, furniture turned into giant plush dolls, and colorful additional rooms added to the immense property. But as alarming as it was to discover a clown holding balloons in the study or a jungle gym taking up the foyer, it wasn't Gabriel's additions that disturbed the Northhalls.

It was the subtractions.

If something scared or upset Gabriel, he'd banish it from existence. First it was inconsequential items – clothes that felt uncomfortable, toys he grew tired of, a plate of broccoli he refused to eat. Soon, entire portions of the house were missing, with only frightening black voids left in their place. The Northhalls did well to instill morals in their son, but as with every child, he had his moments of impulse, confusion, and poor judgement.

The week that Gabriel turned five, a postal carrier named Freddy Alonzo had the unfortunate fate of meeting him at the front door. Gabriel expected a birthday present, but none of the day's packages were for him. In a brief tantrum, Freddy left the world, deleted as if he'd never existed. No one came looking for the man, for he had never been born, nor were his two children or six grandchildren. Only Elena and Warren Northhall remembered Freddy Alonzo, the nice man who'd delivered their mail for seventeen years. The rest of the world hadn't merely forgotten him, for he had never been.

Before the beloved postal carrier could fade from his own mind, Professor Northhall made the hard decision to share his turmoil with the World-Mind Foundation, headquartered four hours south in St. George, Utah. World-Mind was a think tank whose roster included titans of industry and science, geniuses who theorized about the untapped potential of the human brain, the fabric of the universe, and parallel worlds. Northhall had been a prominent member in good standing for decades.

They based all their intellectual debates and discussions on theories until the day Gabriel burst into their lives.

The council at World-Mind unanimously concluded that Gabriel's upbringing must take place at a remote facility, at a location as barren as possible. They considered moving him to the Sonoran Desert in nearby Arizona but concluded it was best to build overseas. The foundation looked to such places as Antarctica, the Sahara Desert, the Siberian Wilderness, Central Australia, and Central Greenland. They finally chose Bolivia for its long, comfortable summers and short, dry, clear winters. With the foundation's connections and financial support, Northhall acquired an abandoned military bunker in the Uyuni Salt Flats. At nearly four-thousand square miles of flat, empty space, the region allowed for seclusion with unobstructed views in all directions.

Northhall soon spirited his adopted son away to the crumbling concrete structure, hundreds of miles from anyone and anything he could see, which was the only known way to control his power. The monumental task of restoring and remodeling the bunker over two years was reduced to a single hour as Gabriel reshaped it into the only home he'd ever known – Northhall Manor.

The professor quickly realized that it wasn't a simple reproduction. Gabriel somehow tied the false mansion to the real one. Anything that existed in the majestic house in Salt Lake City would also exist in its perfect facsimile – every piece of furniture, every board of wood peeling paint, every stone and blade of grass.

Taking an extended leave of absence, Northhall spent two years in Uyuni, raising his son in the perfect duplicate of his estate, frequently returning to America for business with Chambers and World-Mind. Believing that one of the boy's adopted parents needed to move to the salt flats permanently, Elena embraced her role as mother and protector, not only caring for the child but caring for the world, keeping it far from his grasp. Gabriel's view of the cultures and peoples he cherished would forever remain on the pages of books and magazines, carefully curated by his parents.

For ten years, the Northhalls maintained Gabriel as good and moral, keeping his powers in check, knowing that he could never leave the home he'd built for them. Taken from their lifeless surroundings, he dubbed the second home their "oasis on the moon."

But nothing lasts forever, even for a child god. At the start of their eleventh year on the moon, doctors diagnosed Elena with cancer. She and the professor had seen it coming and planned for it by introducing new "friends" to help raise Gabriel. By the time Elena succumbed to the disease, the new team was in place.

Donnamaria Solíz came from the World-Mind council. When asked to dedicate the rest of her life to help raise Gabriel, she saw it as an unprecedented opportunity to study an omnipotent being, the unexplored bridge between science and religion. She moved into the Uyuni mansion and became its chief caretaker.

Troy Walker served as the foundation's Executive Director. He, too, saw Gabriel as a window to another level of existence and eagerly volunteered the rest of his life to become his "big brother" through adolescence and beyond.

Mateo Galvez rounded out the group as its youngest member. A dedicated student of the human condition, Mateo was fascinated by the workings of the vast, untapped mind of young Gabriel, and felt honored to help raise him.

These brilliant scholars fit in well. Gabriel accepted his new "real" friends, a contrast to the false, single-day companions he conjured to educate and entertain him, each fading away come sunset. This new family allowed the professor to continue working and living in Salt Lake City, returning to Uyuni monthly to check in on his son. The team felt Gabriel needed to latch onto those who committed to remaining in the salt flats and to regard his father's presence as a monthly treat. Presumption could turn to complacency, which could easily turn to disaster.

Through years of observation and interaction, the team learned a great deal about Gabriel's power, its scope, and its limitations. Gabriel could only alter what he saw, and could only reshape his immediate environment. For this reason, Uyuni was not just the perfect home for this innocent, benevolent, omnipotent being – it was the only conceivable one.

Everything changed on the morning of Gabriel's thirty-fifth birthday when he found an issue of *Time Magazine* from 1990. Diana, Princess of Wales, smiled on the cover, a genuine princess who was pretty, wealthy, famous, and adored by people all over the world. Curious and fascinated, Gabriel opened the magazine to read about her.

To his surprise, another article about another woman quickly grabbed his interest.

Halfway down page twenty-eight was a column entitled "American Dreamer Spotlight," a human-interest piece about a young woman from a Mexican working-class family in Modesto, California. No princes or castles or riches for her, she shared a bed with two brothers and took care of her grandmother. She worked hard, graduated from college early, and made her way to Chambers University as one of Professor Warren Northhall's five proteges.

"This is where you come in," Northhall said to Ria. "He read about you, saw your picture in *Time Magazine*, and wanted to meet you in person. Our understanding of his power shifted that day."

"His power?" Ria asked, still searching for logic and reason. "You act like he's a god."

"Not exactly," Northhall said. "A god is without boundaries. We can contain Gabriel."

"You sure?" Ria asked. "What if he decides this place isn't enough?"

"He can change it."

"What if he simply walks out the door to roam the Earth?"

Northhall didn't like to think of that prospect. "If my son ever leaves, we wouldn't be able to stop him, this house would disappear, and I'd have no choice but defer to Miguel and Luis and the fifty other guards along the perimeter. But it will never come to any of that. His power restrains itself with rules and limits and relationships."

Relationships.

"One of which is a connection with the original Northhall Manor," the professor said. "Whatever exists in one house exists in the other."

"I gathered that much," she said, still reeling from the revelation.

"From what we observed, he would create something here, and its counterpart would appear back home in Salt Lake. Over years of experiments, we thought we'd pinpointed how it worked. Our understanding flipped on its head when I brought Mister Rufus here."

Mister Rufus?

Why does that sound familiar?

Why does so much of this sound familiar?

Mister Rufus was an old 1940s mohair teddy bear Professor Northhall kept from his childhood. During one of his monthly visits, he brought the weathered, antique plush toy to the Uyuni house, figuring that an item with only sentimental value would benefit a child who could have literally any treasure he wanted at the blink of an eye. Upon handing the ragged bear to Gabriel, a second Mister Rufus appeared on the floor of the parlor in Salt Lake City. Unlike other parallel items, the bear in Salt Lake was new, devoid of the decades of rips and tears and stains.

Further experiments duplicated the result. Anything real that Northhall brought to Gabriel also suddenly existed – new and unblemished – in Salt Lake City.

Having no clue what would happen or how it would affect the fabric of reality, Northhall took the monumental risk of bringing the conjured parallel items to the Uyuni house for Gabriel to enjoy for the day.

"We call them false treasures," Northhall said.

"What do you mean, 'for the day'?" Ria asked.

"We found that a false treasure can remain in its house indefinitely, but it doesn't last long if brought to the other house. Things conjured in Salt Lake had their own life back home but when I brought them here, they only lasted a day."

"They lasted until sunset," Mateo said.

"We're still trying to figure out how it works," Northhall added. "His power is growing exponentially, and we're struggling to keep up."

Ria understood, yet still had a myriad of questions. "Explain to me, 'This is where you come in'."

At the edge of the garden stood Donnamaria, a platter in hand – homemade coffee cake, spring rolls, BLTs, and peach ice tea. She set them down on a picnic table and joined them.

"Now, Warren?" she asked.

"Now," Northhall sighed with a timbre of regret. "Is Troy with him?"

"They're playing a game," she said. "He has Gabriel well occupied."

"Someone tell me why I'm here!" Ria demanded. "Why did Gabriel want to meet me? That magazine story? Was that it?"

"Whatever exists in one house exists in the other," Northhall said. "Anything real here has a false counterpart back home, only new, untouched by tragedy and time. It had always been trinkets, toys, games. But then Gabriel found that magazine."

Gabriel sometimes rummaged through Troy's, Mateo's, and Donnamaria's personal belongings, searching for something new and "real" to entertain him. He recently found an old magazine that contained a story about a young girl who'd worked her way through college and found work in Salt Lake City.

"Yes, yes, we covered that, he read about me," Ria said, still waiting for answers.

Donnamaria stepped forth and tenderly placed her hand on Ria's shoulder, an action she'd wondered about for the past week.

"No," Donnamaria said. "He read about me."

Donnamaria Riveras grew up in the industrial city of Modesto in Central California. She worked her way through college, baking pan dulce at her mother's panadería while carrying a dual major in Experimental Psychology and Behavioral Science at Sacramento State. She achieved a teaching credential and became a fixture there for another ten years.

She met her "rock star" Professor Warren Northhall at a San Francisco conference on Behavioral Medicine. Northhall seemingly had everything she wanted in life, including his new tenure at Chambers University in Salt Lake City, and all the respect and accolades that came with it.

Donnamaria quickly impressed him with her work. By the end of that weekend conference, he'd convinced her to start a new life at Chambers University, both as a postgraduate and one of his proteges. Less than a month later, she moved from Modesto, California to Salt Lake City, Utah.

After apprenticing under Northhall for four years, she married her colleague, Francisco Solíz, and took his name. Soon, a baby boy was on the way. Donnamaria thought her loving family would be her heart's home for the rest of her life. It became her everything, replacing the ambition of following in her mentor's footsteps. But the winds of the world cruelly shifted and threw her headlong into a new life.

During the first rain of a Utah winter, when the roads were slick and traffic not yet acclimated, a rush-hour car crash tragically took Francisco's life. In her torment, Donnamaria miscarried her unborn son, leaving her emotionally lost and alone. Warren and Elena Northhall were always there for her, but she suddenly lacked purpose. There seemed no point in going on.

Still a brilliant scholar with much promise, she found solace with Warren at the World-Mind Foundation. They brought her into their highly classified project: the Northhalls had a young boy with the mental powers of conjuration and environmental manipulation. The foundation had moved the boy to the desolate Uyuni Salt Flats in Bolivia. With Elena Northhall battling breast cancer, the boy would soon need a mother.

Donnamaria needed a child.

So it came to pass, over thirty years ago, that Donnamaria Riveras Solíz made the life-changing decision to dedicate the rest of her life to caring for the special boy, raising him to be a good man in honor of her late husband. Her potential to become Professor Warren Northhall's next grand discovery long behind her, she became consumed with serving as Gabriel's mother figure, forever living in the illusion of a house in the middle of nowhere. The professor, Mateo, and Troy would continue to observe Gabriel, while Donnamaria would genuinely love him.

Everything felt right again.

On his thirty-fifth birthday, Gabriel found the old issue of *Time Magazine* that featured Princess Diana's legacy while merely mentioning young Donnamaria's meteoric rise in the world of Psychology. He fell in love with the photo of the young woman nicknamed "Ria," not realizing it was his surrogate mother. He spoke of her often and wished that she could come to the Uyuni house one day to meet him.

Soon, Ria appeared outside the Northhall Manor in Salt Lake City, on the eve of the professor's farewell party.

Whatever exists in one house exists in the other.

Only newer. Younger. Full of life.

* * *

"I don't understand," Ria said, still grappling with the story she'd been told. "He conjured me? Like that old stuffed bear?"

"He wished to meet Ria Riveras," Northhall said, "not realizing that she was already here and had been taking care of him for decades. So you appeared, two days ago, standing outside my home in the snow by the well. I thought I might see you there eventually, but nearly lost my train of thought when I spotted you in the crowd."

"This can't be!" Ria said. "I have memories! I remember meeting you and moving to Salt Lake City! Every day, working with you for four years, I remember it all!"

"That's how long I was his protege," Donnamaria said, "before I met Francisco."

Ria struggled to comprehend the impossible. She faced her older self. "If we're... the same person... how can we both be here?" The words tumbled out like nonsense as she spoke them. "I thought parallels of real things you brought here... false things... didn't last."

"Sunset," Mateo said with the soft tone of apology. "Whatever the professor brings here from Utah lasts until sunset. It shocked me to see you wake up in the rover this morning."

Ria looked out over the garden, at the endless salt flats that stretched out to the setting sun. She suddenly felt an odd acceptance of her fate, of the brief life Gabriel had granted her.

"Why bring me here?" she asked. "Why not leave me back home where I could live on?"

"Your existence is unprecedented," Northhall said, searching for the words. "Gabriel has never created a fully developed person before. A year ago, he created a limited, adolescent version of Mateo, a mute ten-year-old boy without personality or memories. He stood in the doorway of the Salt Lake house on Christmas morning, confused and scared. We brought him here to meet Gabriel, but he didn't make it through the day. It saddened us to lose him."

Mateo bowed his head, unable to face Ria now.

"We honestly didn't think you'd exist this long," Northhall continued. "My son knew he created you, and he urged us to bring you here. He wanted to meet you before..."

"Before the sun sets," Ria concluded.

"This is unexplored territory. We had to do this. His power grows each day, and we're hoping you're still here when night falls."

The scientist in her understood and knew the truth. "There's no evidence to support the idea that I'll sustain any longer than Mateo's parallel."

"Correct," Professor Northhall said. "In which case, this may be goodbye, my dear."

Donnamaria approached her younger self. "It was wonderful to see you again," she said, wiping away a single tear. "I'd nearly forgotten the bright, ambitious, young woman I once was, the wide open future I had. I'm glad we spared you the heartache of my life."

"It was wonderful to see you, too," Ria said. "At least I got to see how my life turned out. You shouldn't have any regrets. I certainly don't."

"Wherever you're going," Donnamaria said, "say hello to Abuelita Nina if you see her. Tell her I miss her so. Tell her I think of her every day."

"What a funny thing for a scientist to say."

"That scientist is long gone. I leave the studies, the theories, and experiments to Warren and the others. All I have now is Gabriel. My son."

The sun set behind the distant Pallaly Loma mountains to the far west. As day turned to night, young Ria Riveras disappeared, fading with the twilight of the setting sun, leaving the professor, Mateo, and Donnamaria staring at the ground where Ria once stood.

Professor Northhall stepped into the duplicate house, to the parlor near the front entry. He noticed the gold-and-silver gift-wrapped box still sitting untouched on the fireplace mantel. He opened it while he still could and found a sterling silver pocket watch nestled in velvet. From his coat, he pulled out his old pocket watch and held both timepieces in his hands.

They were identical.

The tarnished pocket watch in his left hand was nearly forty years old. The one in his right hand was shiny, brand new. Inscribed on their backings was the same message from his young protege.

> *"Always remember the time we had shared. The Lord grants no greater gift."*

The pocket watch and its decorative box faded from existence.

"I'll always remember," Northhall said.

Seven Blocks to Bridalveil

The walk felt longer each week. From Manny's modest home – the small, crumbling Craftsman bungalow where he was born and raised and destined to remain forever – the weekly trek across the rural town of Bolton formed a giant "L." From his front door, Manny's walk crossed five city blocks, turned south at the police station, passed three more blocks, and ended at Dr. Byrd's office.

Though Manny had spent most of his life in Bolton, he'd never ventured past the doctor's office. It felt like nothing existed beyond.

The mornings before each weekly session, he'd awaken from a dream about his father. Sometimes Casey and Mr. Cervantes were also in the dream, but his father Russell was reliably there, on his knees, turned away, working on his old Monarch lawnmower in his corner of the garage.

Though Manny always set his alarm clock, it never woke him. Casey always did, seconds before the old wind-up brass clock rang. Whether he stood looming over Manny's bed, his six-foot-tall frame blocking the sunlight from the window, or he sat cross-legged at the foot of the bed playing some attempt at solitaire on a pillow, Casey always woke before his brother, shuffling his weathered deck of cards. Though Casey was the older of the two brothers, he didn't fully grasp the rules of solitaire. He never read the rules to his card games, nor could he ever hope to understand them.

"Do you always gotta play cards on the bed?" Manny yawned, irritated. He expected no response from his mute brother, the spitting image of their father even more so than Manny. "Play on the floor. There's more room down there."

Casey ignored the suggestion and kept laying out cards in rows, not quite knowing why. He just liked how they looked in neat, cascading rows, all those pretty kings and queens and jacks. At least he alternated between red and black, that much he understood.

Manny's mornings were a strict routine, and the days he was due at Dr. Byrd's office were no exception. He rose wearily out of bed, faced himself in the mirror, and took his time shaving. He only shaved once a week, so he ensured that his chin and cheeks felt smooth, leaving only his trimmed mustache. Afterward, he put on his clothes, his usual white T-shirt with gray pants.

Casey always dressed before Manny woke, one of the few things he could do on his own. He, too, was a creature of habit, wearing the same Spider-Man shirt, the same baggy jeans, the same worn pair of black-and-white Converse knock-offs, day after day.

Manny combed his thick, coal-black hair in the mirror just before leaving for his walk. He parted his hair to the right and patted down a cowlick that sprung up a minute later, regardless.

"How about staying home this time?" Manny asked Casey, still distracted by his cards. "I mean, you're a big boy, Case. You can take care of yourself for an hour." It was a pointless request. He knew he had to bring Casey, just as he knew that a back-and-forth conversation with the developmentally challenged man-child was impossible. "I guess I'm stuck with you."

Five blocks of neighbors saw Manny walking down Green Street. Casey walked behind him. Their resemblance was striking, almost like seeing twins. They even had the same damn cowlick. Though Manny had been walking to Dr. Byrd's office each week for over a year, he always felt uncomfortable. He imagined all the eyes in Bolton on him, everyone knowing where he was going and why. He knew it was all in his mind but still he felt their stares.

At the corner of the "L," Manny waved at the officers outside the police station as he turned south on Goldenrod Street. One or two officers would sometimes wave back, but most of the time they glanced at him and turned away without a word or gesture. Manny didn't take offense. Far from being a morning person, he assumed the officers didn't want to be there at that hour any more than he did.

Three more blocks and Manny reached Bridalveil Boulevard, where Dr. Emil Byrd's one-room corner office waited for him. Just outside the doctor's door, Manny paused, grabbed his brother by the shoulders, and looked into his eyes. "Case, I want you on your best behavior. Don't distract me while I'm talking to the doctor. Don't walk up to me, and don't offer me a card. Just sit in the corner and play your solitaire. Understand?"

Casey didn't respond. He never did. He awkwardly shuffled the cards in hand, his eyes only on his kings and queens, fanning them out. With a flick of his fingers, he offered Manny the King of Hearts, the only form of direct communication the young man ever displayed. Manny nodded thanks and hoped that his instructions got through, but there was no way of knowing until he sat in Dr. Byrd's office.

"Mr. Valentine," said Dr. Byrd with a warm smile. "Good morning. Please come in and sit anywhere you like." The doctor often referred to him as "Mr. Valentine," particularly at the start of their sessions, as if it were part of a ritual. Despite the formal greeting, Manny had become quite comfortable with the psychologist. Still, hearing his surname spoken aloud made him uncomfortable, though not enough to voice concern.

Being told to choose any seat he wanted felt like a joke considering there was only a wooden corner chair and a couch opposite Dr. Byrd's desk, and given that Manny always chose the couch. Casey sat cross-legged on the floor in front of the corner chair, allowing him to continue his pseudo-solitaire.

Manny always insisted that Casey sit on the floor. "Remember, Case," Manny commanded with a firm tone. "Stay put. Stay sitting on the floor." Casey started laying his cards out on the doctor's Spanish ceramic tile.

"You've brought the big guy again," Dr. Byrd noted. "How's he doing?"

"The same," Manny sighed. "You know he's the same."

"How about you?" Dr. Byrd subtly slid his notepad closer.

"I'm the same, too," Manny said, forcing a smile. "You know I'm the same."

"Do I? Doesn't matter, it's not about me. The main reason you come to see me is to break free from the Same Old Manfred Valentine, right?"

There was his surname again. It stung to hear, especially following his stuffy, full first name, but he let it go. "Yeah, and some days it kinda feels like it's going in that direction, but most days it pulls me back."

"Like the days you're scheduled to meet with me?"

"Yeah. Those days."

"Still having the dreams?" Dr. Byrd asked, picking up a pen. It mean he was about to start fishing.

"This morning, they were all there."

"Wanna walk me through it?"

"What for?" Manny asked. "You already know the dream, Doc. I probably told you fifty times."

"Sure, but it's been a while, and tiny differences can mean a lot. You don't have to give me details if it makes you uncomfortable. Just tell me how you felt and go from there."

"Helpless," Manny said. "Weak. No tiny differences."

"Let's walk it back a little." Dr. Byrd trod carefully whenever Manny began a session so hesitant to share his thoughts. He made a quick note, returned his pen and pad to the desk, and focused squarely on his client, like two friends having a friendly conversation. "We can start from any point you choose. From there, we can ease into the dream from this morning."

"Alright. The garage, maybe? Farther back?"

"Farther back, if you feel up to it."

"Is there coffee in that thing?" Manny asked, pointing to an insulated carafe in the corner behind the doctor. "I didn't have time to stop for a cup." He was nervous, stalling, but he certainly wanted that coffee, another part of their ritual.

Dr. Byrd nodded, smiled, and poured his patient a cup of fresh, black coffee. "Cup of Joe, hot and neat," he said, using Manny's introductory words from their first session a year ago. "You take it the same? Or have your tastes changed?"

"The same. You know I'm the same."

"Just a reminder, it's not about me, what I know or don't know. It's all about how you feel today."

Dr. Byrd slid the coffee across his desk. Manny rose from the couch, picked up the steaming cup, and took in the coffee's aroma for a moment before returning to the couch. "Damn good stuff. Way better than what we get at lunch."

"I keep my machine clean," the doctor said, "and I grind my own beans. Now you know my secrets."

"I guess it's time I share mine."

"Only if you're up to it. Remember, there's never any rush with me. We have plenty of time."

"I suppose we do. Never thought of it like that."

"I hope that's a comfort," Dr. Byrd said.

"Out there, people tell me what to do, when to do it, how to do it. But here in your office, I feel like... I feel like I'm free, if only for an hour."

"In here, you're in charge. You can share with me anything you want or nothing you don't."

"I appreciate that. I feel like our sessions are a gift."

"And I appreciate that," Dr. Byrd said, smiling sincerely. "Most of my patients don't see things the way you do. They see me as judgmental, out to humiliate them, trick them, catch them in a lie, like so many others in their lives. You ever feel that way?"

"Nah, I know you're a good guy, Doc. You're just trying to help. I bet you probably get some real loons sitting on this couch."

"I wouldn't use those words, but sure, many of my patients aren't ready to open up. They're still struggling with pain, fear, regret. That's a big one. Regret. It's why they come here. But let's refocus and get back to you. I'm interested in what you have to say."

Manny sipped his coffee, warm and comforting, like Dr. Byrd and his modestly appointed office. Other than his framed higher education adorning the walls, a few potted plants, and a couple of family photos on his desk, the room was simple and peaceful, a stark contrast to the harsh reality outside those walls.

"How about I go back to the beginning?" Manny offered.

"Great place to begin."

Manny smirked into a slight smile. "I bet you're a real comedian, Doc, you know, in a more social setting."

"Oh, I'm hilarious. But enough about..."

"I know, it's not about you. We're here for me." Manny paused and took a deep breath before taking Dr. Byrd back to his childhood. "Alright then. I guess we'll start with my pop."

Russell Valentine was a giant. He was fat, to be sure, but he was also tall and strong, his large, leathery hands like baseball gloves. From an early age, Russell worked in the fields and trees, something he preferred over the "reading and writing nonsense" they forced on him in school. When he was ten, he picked grapes and red peppers on the family ranch. At fourteen, he dropped out of school to work on a commercial farm and never looked back, never opened another goddamned book. At twenty, he found work at a large nursery, delivering plants and saplings to clients in the suburbs.

Russell's big personality and booming voice came across as rugged and charming in the dirt and sweat of a hard day's work. After a few years, he'd gained the trust of several well-to-do families and went out on his own, poaching them as his clients. With just an old pickup truck, a couple of lawnmowers, and a 55-gallon trash can full of tools, "Valentine Lawn and Garden" served nine neighborhoods in the North End district of town, an area of lavish homes, each dwarfing his family's old Craftsman bungalow.

While Manny's father helped northern families keep up with the Joneses, his mother Yolanda mostly stayed at home. Manny never referred to her as a "homemaker" because he didn't think she deserved anything that sounded like a job title.

After Russell left each day at dawn, Yolanda made her sons' breakfast. If she was there when Manny and Casey woke, the food would be hot, usually eggs and toast, sometimes with sausage links on the side. Classic Rock would play on a small radio above the sink. If she was gone by the time the boys finally wandered out of their shared room, two bowls of shredded wheat and a carton of skim milk awaited them. The radio would be silent like the rest of the house.

Yolanda would often leave minutes after her husband. She'd spend her days gossiping at her friend's salon or serving oatmeal to senior citizens at the community center. Manny would later learn that there were other places his mother would frequent, and that she placed the bowls of shredded wheat on the kitchen table the night before. It was on those days that she left long before Russell rose out of bed.

For years, Manny had his suspicions about his mother. He heard the deadbolt of the front door and the rumbling engine of her Corolla struggling on the winter mornings. But he never pursued his curiosity. He feared that his suspicions would prove true, forcing him to face the reality of his parents' crumbling marriage.

Manny would come to regret his long silence one morning when he and Casey found hot breakfasts wrapped in aluminum foil, an effort Yolanda had never made when leaving the house early. Those covered plates of bacon and eggs and English muffins turned out to be a final loving meal for her boys.

That cold, early morning, still bundled in bed, Manny heard his mother's old Corolla rumble away for the last time. He'd never get the chance to ask her about her days ever again.

Lynn Harrod

Manny had just turned sixteen.

Casey was seventeen.

* * *

"That was the first time I had bacon," Manny told Dr. Byrd. "Ma never made it for us. She sometimes cooked it on weekends, but it was only for the 'working man' of the house. Casey took a piece from pop's plate once and got a backhand to the face."

"I'm sorry to hear that."

"It made me hate bacon," Manny said. "Ironic that it was on the table for us the morning she left. I took a bite and wrapped up the rest. I went with Fruit Loops instead."

"Saved the bacon for your pop?" Dr. Byrd asked.

"Nah. I gave it to Casey. He loved it, thought nothing of it. It was a treat for him. He hoped she'd make more when she came home."

"But you knew the truth."

"I think I knew for a long time."

"How'd that make you feel?"

"Guilty," Manny said, admitting it to himself. Saying the word aloud made him nauseous. "Maybe if I had talked to her more, I mean really talked to her, not just ask her for something, maybe she would have stuck around."

"You know it wasn't your fault, right?" Dr. Byrd asked with a careful tone.

"Sure," Manny assured him. "But knowing it and feeling it are two different things."

"Did your father know right away that she left him?"

"She put a note in his lunchbox so he wouldn't find it until later that morning. By then, she was long out of town."

"How'd he take it?" Dr. Byrd asked.

"Come on, you know how," Manny said, tiring of the doctor's mind game. "Bad. That's how he took it. Real bad."

"Of course, he took it badly," Dr. Byrd said. "Of course, I know how it all went down. Your file is quite detailed. It tells me everything, but it doesn't show me how you experienced it. I need you to tell me in your words, something other than 'bad'."

Manny sighed and continued. "He came home hours late from work, his shirt soaked with rum and beer. He threw his toolbox down in the living room. It stuck a mean gash in the wood floor. That's when Casey asked him when she was coming home to make more bacon. I should have warned him to leave pop alone."

"He was rough with you."

"He slapped Casey around. It took him by surprise. I stepped in and took the beating meant for my brother. I mean, Case was bigger than me, but he wouldn't have taken it well." Manny paused and cleared his throat, failing to hide the lost expression in his eyes. "Look, do I really need to go over this again? Every night was just like that for the next few months. I'd just be repeating myself."

"Alright," Dr. Byrd said, not wanting to push his patient too hard. "We can stop here. I know it's a lot to unpack."

"Thanks, Doc," Manny said, relieved.

"Eventually, though, we have to keep going, all the way to the garage. That's a day I haven't heard before, not from you, anyway. But it doesn't have to be today if you've had enough."

Manny heard his doctor's sincere words, saw the eager interest in his eyes, the way he sat forward in his chair. "I had enough years ago. I guess... it might as well be today."

"I'm here," Dr. Byrd said, comforting him. "I'm listening."

Manny slid his empty coffee cup across the doctor's desk. "Cup of Joe, hot and neat?"

Dr. Byrd poured him another cup and patiently waited, pad and pen now firmly in hand. He was fishing in deep waters now.

Manny sipped his coffee and returned to his past.

* * *

In the three months after Yolanda left the Valentine home, Russell grew increasingly angry with each passing day. He left the house late, not getting out of bed – often the living room sofa – until well past noon.

Manny navigated each day carefully. He knew not to cross his delicate father. Even a glance in his direction could set him off. He told Casey to "give pop a lot of space."

The two teens were essentially on their own. Manny was never taught how to cook, so he served Pop Tarts, peanut butter, or cheese toast for breakfast. In the evenings, he made fried bologna with mustard on white bread. He remained by his brother's side at all times, quitting the soccer team to meet Casey after school and walk him home, fielding awkward questions like "When's ma comin' back?"

Eventually, Manny felt the need to bring his brother to the cruel truth, that it was just them now. Casey felt confused, crushed, and it was Manny's job to control that spiral of emotion on the long walk home so it wouldn't later spill over on their teetering father.

Russell's work dried up. His clients grew tired of his no-shows, of the overgrown Bermuda grass and invading weeds in front of their precious manicured homes. When he was there, his drunken state was offensive and embarrassing. Even when he cut and trimmed their lawns into immaculate squares, they couldn't very well boast about their landscaper when he was seen stumbling around, muttering obscenities, and that seemed to be just as important to them as the quality of his work. Image matters in suburbia.

Manny regretfully never heard his mother's side of things, but had to endure his father's, forced to hear his loud, slurred, bitter summary of their broken family every evening.

Yolanda had met Fernando Cruz, a volunteer at the Bolton Community Center, a tall, lean man with "a red Mustang and a faggot goatee." He got into her head, brainwashed her into becoming his whore. At Fernando's insistence, she took twelve years of marriage and the honor of a family and shoved them in the toilet all to spite her husband who had worked so hard to build a decent home for her. Russell felt glad she left. He didn't want that bitch raising his boys, eating the food he provided, spoiling his bed after disgracing herself with that stuck up, college-degree bastard.

That was Russell's view.

Manny had long since pieced together a different account.

Russell Valentine had always been abusive, drunk or sober. The only difference was whether the abuse was violently physical or a seething verbal tirade. It got to where hearing him curse the day you were born, curse his shitty working-class house on that shitty working-class street, was a sigh of relief compared to what sometimes followed.

From the beginning, Russell forbade his wife from getting a job or seeing her friends and flew into a rage whenever she didn't have fried chicken and potatoes waiting for him after working a thankless job for rich pricks all day. He worked hard to grow his business, but his privileged clientele offered no admiration or respect for his efforts. They simply regarded him as "the gorilla that cuts the grass," a cruel insult Russell overheard once.

Yolanda would have taken her boys with her when she rode off in Fernando Cruz's red Mustang, but she feared the repercussions of such an audacious move. She feared Russell would track her down, harm her, harm her children. She feared that he'd go to the community center to confront Fernando, terrorize him, guns in both hands, escalating the scene to an unimaginable point of no return.

Thus, Yolanda Valentine made the heartbreaking decision to leave town with Fernando Cruz and never look back, deciding that her boys should remain behind to care for their disturbed father and hopefully help him move on. They were nearly men, after all, and would surely be out of the house soon.

That was Manny's view.

Everything changed, confronting him with frightening focus on the first Saturday of April, late morning, three months after his mother left town. Russell sat in the garage with their neighbor, Mr. Cervantes, repairing his last working mower, the old Monarch he started with back when he first left his secure nursery job to go out on his own.

Manny was weeding along the back fence.

Casey was playing solitaire on the patio.

Mr. Cervantes arrived to lend Russell some tools along with unsolicited advice on engine repair. He ran his own lawn care business, serving small businesses and new housing developments along with the plush contract of caring for the landscapes of the city's municipal offices as the proverbial cherry on top. A city contract is the Holy Grail for blue-collar men in their line of work, a juicy, guaranteed paycheck every week for years at a time.

Whenever Manny saw Mr. Cervantes with his father, it gave him a moment of relief. Despite being competitors, Russell acted on his best behavior in the presence of the successful peer he so envied. Talking shop with him seemingly as equals while stooped over an old Monarch mower was Russell's own version of Keeping Up With the Joneses. Over the course of a shared six-pack, he felt prosperous and respected again.

Upon seeing Mr. Cervantes leave, the brief respite gone, Manny doubled his efforts weeding at the back fence. He wanted to finish his chores before his father came over to scold him for working slowly or cutting the grass unevenly or any other "disrespect" he could find.

Casey walked over, shuffling a deck, and asked his brother to pick a card. Manny normally chose a card and feigned surprise when Casey "guessed" it, but that morning Manny felt frustrated and annoyed, the months and years of walking on eggshells around their father finally overcoming him. He barked at his big brother to leave him be, to allow him to finish his work.

"Casey! If you're not gonna work like a man, at least stay out of my fuckin' way!" Manny never felt more like his father's son than he did that moment, and that undeserved, chastising rebuke would haunt him forever.

Casey's simple mind didn't register the rage. He merely shrugged and retreated to the garage.

A minute later, Manny realized his brother was not within eyesight. He heard his father curse, followed by a piercingly loud clatter of metal on cement. Before he could think of what might have happened, he sprinted to the garage.

Manny turned the corner and halted at the open garage door. His body and mind failed him as he stood motionless, taking in the silent, grim scene that would scar him for life.

His father sat on one of his broke-down riding lawn mowers, rocking back and forth, his face in his palms. Casey laid curled on a large oil stain embedded in the cement floor. The six-foot stain, a stark contrast of black on pale gray, served as his brother's deathbed, growing larger as blood poured out from his face.

The cold realization rushed into Manny as he bent down and shook his brother, the realization that he was not waking up from his father's wrath. Not this time. His brother's death had been as quick and sudden as the crash he heard moments before.

Casey's cards laid scattered across his father's worktable, a few face-up on the darkened cement.

"I told that boy to play on the floor," Russell murmured pathetically, not daring to look at either of his sons. "He didn't listen. He didn't respect me."

Manny didn't need an explanation. Eyeing a mower blade at his feet, spattered with blood, the scene played out in his mind with pristine clarity.

Moments before, his father knelt beside his decrepit mower in the corner, bitter at having just heard Mr. Cervantes jabber on about his new fleet of trucks, his new crew, his new fucking city contract, his sons in college, and his loving wife's new Lexus. Casey wandered in after being chased away by his brother and quietly laid out his solitaire on the worktable, stretching rows of alternating black and red cards between tools and lubricants and engine parts.

Russell rose from his Monarch with the detached lawnmower blade in hand, a flat, thick, twenty-one-inch bar of heavy-gauge steel. He fumed at seeing all those kings and queens and jacks laying rank-and-file through his organized storm of work. It was enough to send the man-on-edge far and away from reason.

Russell screamed, "Clean up this fucking mess!" in a rage as he wildly swung the heavy blade in a wide arc. The sharpened edge struck Casey squarely in the forehead, nearly splitting it in half, sending the mentally challenged teenager to the oily cement in an instant death.

Russell knew it was instant. He didn't bother to check on his older son or call out to his younger one. Instead, he slumped, defeated and helpless, onto the seat of his lifeless Monarch across the garage. He sat turned away, his head buried in his hands.

Manny rushed to the phone to call 911, knowing that it was pointless even as he urged the operator to send help. "There's been an accident!" he shouted. "My brother needs a doctor!" His mind spun as he struggled to recall their address, the color of the house, the white pickup truck parked in the driveway.

Upon hanging up the phone, Russell faced him for the first time that morning. "It was an accident, Manny," Russell said in a near-whisper. "It was just an accident. This wasn't supposed to happen. Don't you go tellin' any different. Don't you bring more misery to this damn house."

Twelve minutes later, medical technicians arrived and made an unspoken diagnosis with their defeated expressions. If Casey was somehow still alive before the EMTs parked in the driveway, he was surely dead by the time they slid him past the rear double doors of the ambulance.

Manny had just turned sixteen.

Casey was seventeen.

* * *

Four years after the death of Casey Valentine, four years after a funeral without their mother present, a funeral where neighbors comforted Manny and Russell with absurd notions like "God needed another angel" and "Sometimes bad things happen to good families," after a painful wake at the Bolton Community Center where photos of Fernando Cruz and Yolanda Valentine serving oatmeal to old folks hung mockingly on the walls, Manny's uneasy suspension of disbelief cracked.

He'd convinced himself that his father's version of events had to be true, or perhaps harbored a grain of truth, which was just enough for him to stamp down his sorrow. Mr. Cervantes had confirmed with authorities that Russell Valentine seemed perfectly calm and courteous only moments before as they spoke of lawnmower engines and their strapping teenage sons and the maintenance of Bermuda grass. Surely, Russell didn't intend to end his older son's life. Surely, it was indeed an accident. But a tragedy so easily preventable proved a hard pill for a distraught teenager to swallow.

Manny and his father needed to move on, and a story that no one fully believed – no one who knew Russell Valentine well – would have to suffice. Manny needed to forgive his father somehow. Instead, he came to learn that time does not always heal all wounds, as he was told so many times. He realized that a neglected wound, forever gaping and bleeding in the absence of remorse and compassion, can fester in time with unchecked rot and decay.

Over four years of helping his father rebuild his lawn care business and their shared life, years of continued drunken rants and dishes thrown and late-night, violent, self-pity anguish, Manny's willful ignorance gave way to fiery resentment and overwhelming guilt. Manny let his childlike big brother out of his sight once. He left him alone with his tempest of a father once. He selfishly put himself above Casey once. Manny knew all too well, having replayed every detail of that day in his head hundreds of times, that Heaven was overflowing with poor unfortunate souls who took a misstep only once.

As his brother and sole protector, it was Manny's fault that Casey died. As the only witness to his brother's demise, it was Manny's fault that his unfeeling father never paid for his crime.

Over four years of living with his tormenting guilt drove Manny to contemplate making amends with what could have been, what should have been. Each birthday passed as a heartless reminder of that tragic day, of his cowardly outburst and inaction that led to Casey's death at the hands of their monstrous father.

And so it came to be, on an early fall morning in Downtown Bolton, riding in Russell's work truck, on their way to tend to another wealthy man's perfect lawn in front of his perfect house that sheltered his perfect family, twenty-year-old Manfred Valentine sat silently in the creaking passenger seat, sliding his hand on a black-and-silver Smith and Wesson 642 in his coat pocket as he gazed at his stone-faced father behind the wheel. He'd stolen the compact gun from Paul Angelino, a high school friend who graduated a year early, around the time that Manny dropped out to mow lawns for life.

He was indeed his father's son.

As their wheezing old truck rumbled down Green Street, turning south on Goldenrod Avenue, Manny clutched the pistol in his coat. It felt hot, ready to explode, and it was all Manny could do to keep it from firing incessantly on its own.

"Not today," he thought, as he'd told himself many mornings in that truck. "One day, but not today." His resolve evaporated when his father spoke the unspeakable to his last living kin.

"It's Casey's birthday," Russell said.

"Yep." Manny could think of nothing more to add.

"Too bad he ain't here." Russell brought the truck to a stop, his eyes on the red traffic light before them. "He'd be twenty-one now, strong as an ox. He may have been stupid, but he had muscle."

"Yep." Manny wanted to scream.

"We could've used him on the North End. More manpower would've gotten us into that new Brookside development. We coulda used that money. Too bad he fuckin' checked out early."

Red turned green and Russell continued down Goldenrod.

Manny's hidden pistol felt blisteringly hot.

A few blocks down the road, another light turned red. Russell came to a stop at Bridalveil Boulevard, an upscale shopping district that Manny had never visited, nor had he ever ventured past. The suburbs beyond, including the new Brookside neighborhood, were another world, one that forbade check-to-check families like theirs.

A police sedan faced them across the intersection, also waiting for the red light. During that eternal traffic stop, Russell turned to his son for the first time in months and uttered what would be his last words.

"Point is, the big dumbass left us," Russell said. "We're one man down and that's that. You better work your ass twice as hard or else you'll be checking out, too."

The Smith and Wesson 642 flew out from Manny's coat pocket, its barrel staring Russell dead in the eye, and blasted three shots point-blank to his forehead.

With Russell's foot off the brake pedal, the truck slowly wandered into the intersection, stopping oncoming traffic, coming to a gentle stop against the brick wall of a corner office. Russell Valentine remained upright, eyes open wide, hands locked on the wheel, as his cursed soul fled for Manny to see. The blood streaming down his face resembled tentacles, keeping his skull firmly against its headrest.

Manny exhaled and looked past his dead father to a young man sitting on a bus stop bench outside the corner office.

It was Casey, shuffling his deck of cards, oblivious to the carnage and the police sedan that chirped and beeped as it rushed into the intersection.

"I did it, Casey," Manny said. "He can't hurt us no more."

"Don't move!" Officer Martin yelled from beside the sedan, his gun raised.

Paul Angelino's Smith and Wesson 642 instantly whipped around on its own, Manny's finger firmly on the trigger, and fired two shots at the officer.

The first bullet struck Officer Martin's right arm.

The second bullet struck his right eye.

* * *

Dr. Byrd knew all the details. He'd read the police report many times, combed over the milestones of Manny's life, leading to the fateful moment of his father's murder in the unforgiving daylight of that fall morning. However, today was the first time he'd seen it unfold in its entirety through Manny's eyes.

"Our time's up, Mr. Valentine," he said with a regretful tone. "We'll have to continue next week. I have another patient coming." The state only allotted Manny one hour of therapy a week, a gift that few inmates received. Perhaps the system took pity on him. Perhaps they saw potential in his rehabilitation. "You made a breakthrough today. I want you to know that."

Manny looked behind him at "Casey," the specter of his big brother, still sitting on the floor in the corner of Dr. Byrd's office, playing some attempt at solitaire. Manny had continued to care for him daily long after he buried him, after everyone had somehow accepted his death and the "accident" that caused it. He saw him sitting cross-legged on the front lawns of the North End mansions, watched over him at the kitchen table during his father's ongoing, lonely rants. He cared for him on the morning of the brutal double-murder on Bridalveil Boulevard, and he soon carried him tenderly into Bolton Penitentiary, where he would continue to be his brother and sole protector for the rest of his life sentence.

"Thank you," Dr. Byrd said.

"For what?"

"For opening up and letting me in. I know it's not where you want to be, but it's real and it's the first step to coming to terms with your past."

Casey rose to his feet, the white laces on his Converse knock-offs loose as always, the faded Spider-Man shirt spattered with fresh blood from the cruel gash across his forehead. He approached his brother and fanned out his cards, silently asking Manny to pick one.

Dr. Byrd saw Manny look away, knowing he was looking at his big brother. He quickly held out a plastic bottle of Chlorpromazine, an antipsychotic drug prescribed for schizophrenia, something he'd been urging Manny to consider. It would help him think more clearly and subdue the intense hallucinations that gripped his every waking hour.

"You've come so far during our sessions," Dr. Byrd pleaded. "Now you can go a little further. Please take this."

"I still don't see why I'd want to," Manny said.

"Please take it, Manny."

With Dr. Byrd's Chlorpromazine to his right and Casey's fan of playing cards to his left, Manny contemplated the gravity of his choice, a decision he'd been struggling with for months.

He reached out and picked the King of Hearts.

The walk back from Dr. Byrd's office felt longer each week. The trek through Bolton Penitentiary was a giant "L." Manny's walk crossed three cell blocks, turned west at the guard station, passed five more cell blocks, and ended at Manny's bunk.

Long Green Smile

Joseph W. Hatley's calfskin wingtips made a solid, satisfying sound as he walked into the office, his footsteps transitioning from plush Berber carpet to walnut maple hardwood. The acoustics changed as well, the angled walls and textured ceiling giving his movements perfect volume and clarity, making for a grand entrance. Few would appreciate or even notice such extravagant, indulgent details which belied the otherwise simple office, but they stood out to Joe like neon signs that read "power."

"Good morning," he said as he entered the office from a lengthy wait in the reception room. "I'm Joe, your potential client."

"It is indeed a good morning," said Mr. Drake from behind his desk. "I'm Lukas, your potential consultant."

"Now that the appetizers of first names and good mornings are done, let's get to the steak and potatoes of business." Joe's poker face and tone always felt perfect as he took control of a meeting. He'd become an icon in his field. "Hatley could sell sand to an Arab," his associates boasted.

He would certainly need every fiber of his legendary confidence today.

"Please have a seat, Mr. Hatley. Join me in a cup of coffee? Something a little harder, perhaps. Cuban dark rum? I have a 25-year-old Flor De Cana Centenario that's never been poured."

"No, thank you so much... how did you know my last name?" Joe took his hands out of his pockets, a nervous tell he caught himself doing whenever he felt any uncertainty. "And how did you know my drink?" It had been years since Joe felt such unease in a meeting, and it took him by surprise. Less than a minute in and he was already at a disadvantage.

"I've never met a man who considered such a rare spirit 'my drink,'" Mr. Drake said. "My compliments to your exquisite taste."

The warm flattery did nothing to calm Joe. Knowing that he preferred Cuban dark rum would have been enough to seize his attention, but his wife Margarit gave him a bottle of the quarter-century Flor De Cana Centenario for their twentieth anniversary a month prior. They shared the rum while sitting on a cliff overlooking the Caribbean Sea. With the bottle empty and tossed to the crashing waves below by sunrise, no one else could have known about it.

Mr. Drake stepped to a small wet bar beside his desk and poured himself a cup of coffee, delighted as he savored it, his black suit and slicked black hair matching his drink. "You'll forgive the obligatory offerings. I've apparently made it something of a habit. Beverage before business. I guess I take my time with the 'appetizers.'"

"Again, how did you know my last name?" Joe said, finding it more difficult to conceal his nerves.

"This disturbs you?"

"Not disturbed, just curious," Joe said, trying to convince himself as well as his host. "I didn't make an appointment. The receptionist didn't ask for my name. And I'll be honest, I didn't decide to come here until half an hour ago."

Lukas Drake smiled as he spoke, the type of smile that encompassed an entire face. "I understand your apprehension. Robert called me last night and said that he recommended me to one of his associates. He told me your name, and a few other things about your dilemma. The rest I gathered myself."

Upon that, Joe Hatley felt more comfortable, as if he could still take control of the exchange. He opted to sit on the plush sofa by the window rather than one of the chaise lounges in front of his host's opulent desk. He wanted to feel more relaxed with the business at hand. A couch seemed less formal, plus the large office window provided a view of all Manhattan.

"I've never been up this high in a building before," Joe said in his futile attempt at disarming Drake with modest small talk. He unbuttoned his blazer, another attempt at seeming more at ease. "My building is only twelve stories. I bet your overhead is murder."

"Interesting choice of words. And yes, leases are more outrageous the higher your floor is. I call them leeches. But I have more than enough clientele. They cover my expenses without worry." The consultant returned to his seat behind his desk, sipping his coffee, granting Joe the next word.

"And what do I call you?" Joe asked, still a little edgy about what they were to transact that morning. "Lukas? Luke? Drake?"

"Lukas Drake Vincent, if you're formal. 'Mr. Drake' sounds nice, or 'Mr. Vincent.' Some call me 'Mr. V.' Whatever is easiest on your tongue. I've never considered what people call me very important."

"What else do you know about me, Mr. Drake? I mean, besides my name and my specific drink of choice."

"Quite a lot, actually." Mr. Drake opened a file and glanced at it for a moment before tossing it onto his desk. "Joseph Wilson Hatley, born in Oxmill, Texas, October 1952. Graduated from Kingsville University, 1973. Joined RKA Foods, 1975. Left to start your own company, 'Nature-Born Juices,' 1987. Married to Margarit Hatley 2001. No kids. Might I add that if you had kids, they'd be drinking Nature-Born Juice, because everyone else on the globe is. Including me. You've built quite the empire, Mr. Hatley."

"Creating an empire isn't always an open road on a clear day. It surely wasn't for me. I assume you know why. You seem to know everything else."

"You're referring to your silent partner who has not been very silent as of late?" Mr. Drake said, flashing his smile. "Yes, I know about him. My investigations are thorough. I know you grew your company from a garage operation to the household name it is today, and I know about your difficult partner, Mr. Henry Mitchell, or 'Hank' as his friends and mistresses call him."

"Mr. Mitchell," Joe said with a grunt. "I've called him 'Mitchell' from the night we first met until this very morning." Mr. Drake's incessant smile unnerved Joe. "But go on, Mr. Drake. What else did your crystal ball tell you about him? I mean, besides his well-known Podunk nickname."

"Crystal ball," Drake said with a laugh. "I know Mr. Mitchell was an initial investor at first, but has become very greedy and manipulative. I also know, which you only suspect, that he intends to take over nearly all the stock in a vicious blindside. The notions of illegal dealings and forged documents are not beyond his willingness or ability. Without my help, your best-case scenario is bankruptcy, while your worst-case scenario is rotting in jail by the year's end. You'll no longer be a rising star of industry. You'll be a man in ruin."

"You know all this?" Joe said in a sweaty near-panic, his corporate bravado tumbling away. "Are you sure? Or is this just speculation?"

"Don't forget who you're talking to, Mr. Hatley," Mr. Drake said. "I make it a point to know everything. I'm never unsure, never guessing. But of all the things about my potential clients, the one thing I don't know right away is the service requested. To be blunt, Mr. Hatley, what is it exactly that you want from me?"

Joe couldn't answer immediately. In his heart, he knew what he wanted. He always knew. But he'd never expressed it in anything other than a thought. Though he had no intention of forgetting his agenda, he found it difficult to say the words. "I want Mitchell... out of the way."

"Out of the way?" Mr. Drake asked. "You want him in an office farther down the hall? Moved to another state? His parking space moved three floors beneath yours? What do you mean by 'out of the way'? I have to be sure I understand you correctly."

"I want him eliminated." Joe said, blurting out the words, feeling a sting in his throat.

"Let me help focus your thought. You want him dead."

"Yes."

"And you want me to kill him."

"Yes," Joe said with a quiver in his voice. "I can't have him running the company or putting me in a corner, or any of the outrageous things you claim are in the works. I've worked too hard just to have the crook steal it all away. It was one thing to have him siphoning most of the money for himself, but ownership of my company is entirely different. That's what I truly care about, not the money."

"What a strange thing for a rags-to-riches man to say," Mr. Drake noted.

"I never wanted him as an investor to begin with," Joe confessed, noticing his words almost pouring out now. "But I was young and eager. It had been a long, difficult labor, and I wanted my baby born. Sure, Mitchell dipped a fortune into helping the company get off the ground. But he'd be nowhere without me. He'd be nothing more than a TV-commercial lawyer in a small town, running down ambulances, defending welfare bums with fake whiplash cases."

"Please, Mr. Hatley," Drake said, still sipping his coffee. "Save your anger for later. You'll need it. For now, we should concentrate on the deed. Spell out exactly what you want."

"I want Mitchell dead. Tonight. That's all there is to spell." Joe noticed his reflection in the window, as if seeing another man entirely, his face expressing shock at his vile commands coming forth.

"Don't make it sound so simple, that's actually quite a tall order. A murder within less than a day's notice, my, my."

"This disturbs you?" Joe said, as if to regain control of their chess match. "Is it too much for Lukas Drake Vincent?"

"No, I'll accept the task. I merely ask that you not trivialize the concept of death. Stop to consider that I might find it insulting, and insulting me could be a mistake, as you might imagine."

Joe remembered who he was dealing with, how Robert had frighteningly described him the night before, and how foolishly he'd dismissed it as hyperbole. He suddenly felt the proper fear claw through him, sealing him motionless to the sofa. During his verbal tirade and opening of long-kept emotions, he forgot Drake's horrid, true identity, if Robert was to be believed. "What's your fee, Mr. Drake?" Joe asked, shaking, almost becoming ill, his bluster all but spent.

"My fee. Yes, that needs discussion."

"Is it my soul?" Joe asked unbelievingly. It sounded absurd, but that's the abstract cost Robert had warned him about. "Will you be collecting my soul when I die, or sooner than that?"

Mr. Drake laughed, lips pressed in an amused murmur. It sent a chill through Joe. "Do you believe what your associate told you about me?"

"I think I'm starting to," Joe said, seeing his host in a new light. The angled walls closed in, filling him with dread. "That is the going rate, isn't it? One wish, one soul?"

Drake sighed and shook his head. "To grant a request in exchange for a human soul? That's only in children's storybooks, and the truth behind those stories is always much darker. Think of Humpty Dumpty."

"The egg man from the nursery rhyme?"

"Ah, but he was never actually described as an egg, was he?"

Joe recited the rhyme in his head. "I... I suppose not."

"He was inspired by a fat village idiot in 1630 who fell off a wall in Painswick and cracked open his skull for all to see. The village guard couldn't save him. I know because I was there. His childish egg shape was yet another embellishment of folklore. The fool's tale later inspired the Royalists when they named a cannon after him in 1648, during the English Civil War. It also sat on a wall, this one in Colchester, and tumbled down as the wall was blown apart by Parliamentary forces. The Royalist soldiers couldn't salvage their great weapon, and they perished in the struggle. I know because I was there, too."

Joe wondered what other moments of death and pain Lukas Drake had personally witnessed across history. Maybe all of them.

"Likewise, in my many lifetimes, not once did I request someone's soul as payment. I don't need to. The fact is, I have an overabundance of them."

Mr. Drake saw the building terror in his client's eyes, the growing belief and acceptance, and he preyed on it, enjoying the poor man's torment like a plaything. He stood to look out of his ninety-story window to the canyon of skyscrapers that led to him. His words and manner were unnervingly without emotion, and he paused to offer Joe a moment of contemplation.

"So, what do you want?" Joe asked, confused, afraid of the answer. "What could as man like me possibly offer a man like you?"

"The fee for my services is exactly half of your net worth."

"Half?" Joe asked, sure that he had misheard.

"And since I estimate you to be worth approximately 600 million American dollars, my fee is around 300 million. We'll work out the odd change later."

Joe snapped out of his fear, superstition, and hesitation upon hearing the dollar amount, the businessman in him standing up. "Half? You're out of your mind! I can get a hitman or a common street thug to kill Mitchell! Hell, maybe that's what I should do!"

"The kill is the simple part, Mr. Hatley," Drake said in a calm anger, bending down to speak within inches of Joe's face. "Don't waste life-changing deeds on the stupid and the ignorant. I am no back-alley hitman. I do more than just deal with your business partner. I deal with the aftermath, all the messy bits and pieces that float around when you commit to something like murder. As I stressed before, do not make the mistake of trivializing death in front of me."

Mr. Drake crept down onto the sofa next to Joe, his body slinking unnaturally like a snake, satisfied with the renewed terror he instilled in his client. He held a cigar under his nose and took in its aroma along with the pungent, succulent fear filling the room.

"Under my services, your partner will die tonight as you requested. In addition, I will cleanse you of all guilt about it. Furthermore, though you may be the only person with any real motive to kill Mitchell, the police will never approach you with a single question. They won't even suspect you. No one in this world will conceive of the notion that you had anything to do with it, and no relative of his shall come forth as an heir. No one from the Mitchell Family will protest or step in to take over. All of this comes with the package. I deal mostly in the cleanup of a task, as opposed to the task itself. These are things no 'street thug' can do for you."

Joe thought about Mr. Drake's precise words. No more games, no more innuendo, no more suggestions of who he is or what he's capable of.

Joe Hatley now sat in front of his host as a firm believer.

"If my fee is still beyond your courage, you're free to try your mafioso and ghetto gang punks. Of the two men in this office, it pains me to remind you that it is you who needs me. I've sold my services to kings and countries, countless religions created, corrupted, and destroyed by my hand. I've shaped the histories of whole peoples and cultures and caused more suffering than you can ever comprehend. So, if you want your company back again, your stolen self-esteem and dignity returned, allow me the simple pleasure of plucking Mr. Mitchell from your life. You told me yourself moments ago, all you care about is the company, not the money."

"But what do you need money for? You're the... the..."

Mr. Drake smiled as he pursed the cigar between his lips, lighting it aflame with his fiery breath. "What is it we say about money? What is it the root of? Mr. Hatley, you of all people know that the physical world revolves around the Long Green. Business is the engine of society, a machine whose intake is greed and whose output is power, all fueled by money. The Man Upstairs runs this world like a garden commune. I run it like a business. And souls? They're flimsy. They make for poor bargaining. If you think about it, you'd still belong to me even if you hired some young punk to get your partner 'out of the way.'"

Joe felt confused, not expecting something so assured, so high-stake. He hadn't known what awaited him when he felt compelled to drive to the address on the business card Robert had given him thirty minutes before. He oddly felt he should have been grateful, though, for his eternal soul was worth any amount of money. The decision became clearer with every minute. "You say that Mitchell has plans for me?"

"Many plans," Mr. Drake said, "and I guarantee he will execute those plans without the hesitation you are showing now. You can always plead self-defense on Judgement Day." Mr. Drake returned to his overlord's view of the city.

After a long silence in thought, Joe stood and walked to his host by the window, his hand held out. "Mr. Drake, it looks like we're in business. 300 million, or whatever the exact amount works out to."

Drake grinned and shook Joe's hand. "Done." He snapped his fingers, took a puff of his cigar, sipped the last of his coffee, and sat behind his grand desk again.

"How do I pay you?" Joe asked. "When do I..."

"I'll take care of all the arrangements. It's a simple matter of transferring the funds to my accounts. Nothing unusual."

Drake's calm demeanor about their deal took Joe aback. He had so many questions that he didn't know how to ask. "I'm sorry if I seem disoriented, but I keep expecting something, I don't know what, a cloud of smoke, maybe, or a bolt of lightning. I can't help feeling as though I should be different somehow from a minute ago, before I hired you to kill a man for me. But I feel exactly the same."

"On December 31st, you're Joseph Hatley. When it turns midnight, you're still Joseph Hatley, even though the year has turned."

"There's a difference between New Year's Eve and murder."

"Not to me," Drake said, "and not to you. Not anymore. You won't feel any remorse. I take care of all the messy bits, remember?"

Joe searched himself for any ill feelings, but there were none, just as Drake had said. "Maybe it's because I haven't actually seen or confirmed his death yet."

"No, it's not that, but you will get your confirmation for it will be you that does the deed."

"Me?" Joe said in surprise. "What do you mean?"

"Again, I tend to the cleanup, not the task. That brings up another myth about me. Contrary to what they say, I've never killed anyone or anything. I leave that to desperate men. They seem at home with such acts."

"But I can't kill anyone! I won't! I'm incapable of it! That's why I'm hiring you!"

"Don't underestimate yourself," Mr. Drake told his client. "You are certainly capable of murder. That's the service I've provided. You will kill him as you would a bug under your boot. You won't feel guilt, you won't get caught, and no one will suspect you. Joseph Hatley could stab Hank Mitchell with a kitchen knife sixty times in front of an entire precinct of cops and never get pinned for it."

"You sound so certain," Joe said, astonished.

"What do you think causes injustice? Why do you think innocent men go to the gas chamber while heartless fiends walk the streets? Realize that I don't directly cause any crimes. I never have. I merely allow people the ability to cause them very... how shall I put it... efficiently. Ironic, isn't it? That the Devil Himself is incapable of sin."

"I think I see what you mean."

Drake snuffed his cigar in an ashtray on his desk. "So, I suppose you'll be off to take care of business now. The 'steak and potatoes.'

We shook hands. There are no refunds. There's no need since you won't be changing your mind about this."

"No, that I won't. I'll probably wait until after dinner before I kill him. I'm torn between stabbing him or shooting him. Maybe a good strangling. It'll come to me, I just need some time." Joe said, listening to his long-harbored, morbid fantasies coming alive. "This is amazing, I'm planning to murder someone and I'm approaching it as if I were going to the store for a carton of milk."

"Doesn't it feel good?"

Joe thought for a moment, feeling all novelty slip away. "Yes, it does feel good. I feel like I could kill anybody one-two-three. Just another action, another simple gesture."

"Worth 300 million?" Mr. Drake asked with his wide smile.

"Oh yes, very much worth it. I see that now."

"That's what all of my clients say once the deal's made. It's like a feeling of freedom."

Joe rose to his feet. "Before I leave, I must know, what exactly do you do with your money?"

"I give it out to those who need it. Being good costs nothing, but being evil is usually expensive. Kids in gangs need to have guns and drugs sold to them by someone usually their age. All that money has to come from somewhere. Hate groups and extremists need their weapons. They hold meetings, organize events, run for high office. And we can't forget wars. That's where most of my money goes. I don't know where yours will go just yet, but who knows? 300 million is a lot of Long Green. You might fund the next Hitler."

Joe walked toward the door, thinking about what Drake said. In his mind, he saw the logic in what was explained to him and felt at ease with it. "I never pictured The Devil to be so tangible, so clear and precise, nothing vague."

"What you label God and Heaven is what's incomprehensible," Drake explained. "It would be arrogant for someone to claim that they relate to or understand such things. Men can never truly answer all the questions regarding the concept of omnipotence or the meaning of life. I'm what you'd call a byproduct of all that, leftovers from when The Man Upstairs made the universe. I'm the mess left in the kitchen after He baked a beautiful cake, attracting cockroaches because no one bothered to clean up. And because I'm only a small fraction of existence, it's easy to grasp me. We dismiss kindness every day, but whenever there's evil, everyone turns to look. You want to see it, whether you're watching a mass shooting on the evening news or passing a car wreck on the side of the road."

With a small grin, Joe walked out of Mr. Drake's office. His foot in the doorway, stepping onto the Berber carpet of the reception room, he turned with a final thought. "There's gotta be more to this. In every story I've read and every tale I've heard, there's always a drawback to dealing with The Devil. There's always a catch."

Mr. Drake smiled at his client. "The person you are now is quite different from the person who walked into my office earlier, yet you don't feel a thing. Do you understand?"

"No," Joe said in contentment.

"That's the catch. Good day, Mr. Hatley."

On that last word, Joe walked out with a peaceful look about him. As he left the office, he noticed a nervous young woman sitting in the waiting room, waiting for her appointment with Mr. Drake. How funny it seemed to see someone so apprehensive, so confused.

Joe went home to have his dinner that evening, a Porterhouse steak with Kennebec potatoes, before paying a late-night visit to Mr. Mitchell's family.

The Holy Corridor

Before that cold, drizzling night, Benjamin Stoll had never dared step foot in a wealthy neighborhood, much less wandered the gilded halls of its largest mansion. His footsteps echoed across the marble floor as he passed Impressionist paintings on the walls and Greek statuary in alcoves. It all felt strange, for such extravagant homes never seemed real to the old man. They adorned the covers of magazines he fished out of the trash, were prominently featured in movies he snuck into, or sat beside distant lakes and woods as he watched them slowly drift away in the night from his view atop a freight train. During his lifetime in the wild, living in back alleys and dark corners day by day, Ben often wondered what kinds of elitist pricks lived in such garish, decadent, miniature kingdoms. He never expected to find his old friend lording over one of them.

"Charlie, I ain't never seen digs like this," Ben said as he entered the stately room, one of dozens in the immense house. His raspy voice matched his torn, soiled overalls and unkempt gray hair. "I mean, not for old buzzards like us, anyway. But hey, that fancy suit fits you good, Charlie."

"When you're living on the run," his host said without emotion, "I suppose you don't get to see many grand foyers, parlors, or 'fancy' suits."

Charles Goldwine sat cross-legged in his plush evening chair and spoke with a tepid smile and an almost monotone voice, the riches of this world no longer amusing him. His custom Parisian suit and Italian shoes were now just bits of cloth, his collection of jewelry only baubles, and his sprawling home that used to serve an oil baron's family now stood as a big, pretty box on a hill with eighteen bedrooms kept pristine and pointless, for no one slept in their goose down feather four-poster beds or embraced the sunrise from their private balconies.

"Forget foyers, I ain't seen the insides of *any* rooms for a while," Ben said, forcing a laugh.

"Including haberdasheries, judging from your mess of an ensemble." Charles rose from his leather chair and walked to his liquor cabinet. "Remind me to take care of those rags later."

"You got nice booze, nice clothes, nice house," Ben said. He looked at his host but could still sense the two mouth-breathing gorillas standing along the wall behind him. "I guess money buys new friends, too, eh?"

"The imposing gentlemen standing behind you aren't friends, but they can be compared to my liquor and wardrobe. Each one is the finest money can buy, unique, serving only me."

Charles's bodyguards stood thirty feet apart, each near one of the two doors in the room, quiet and still as though living for his next command. Ben felt uncomfortable in their presence when he entered the house just ten minutes before, a feeling that paled next to the terror he felt when the large men shook him awake at half past midnight and dragged him out of his cardboard tent beneath the freeway overpass.

"Your finest gave me a good scare," Ben said. "I thought I was having a bad trip from tainted crystal, even when they dropped your name. Now, standing here with you in a golden palace like this, I figure it's too goddamn crazy even for a meth fever dream. But hey, your boys found me, so here I am."

"My 'boys' didn't find you," Charles said. "I found you, as difficult as it was. I located you months ago when you were bunkered down in the maw of a Chicago homeless shelter, living off the State of Illinois for as long as possible before you had to run away again, always running, hopping on trains and semi-trucks bound for anywhere else in the wee hours. Can't put down roots and risk revealing your identity, now can you?" Charles swung open the stained glass doors of his liquor cabinet and eyed the rows of antique bottles. "Magnificent, aren't they? I've been collecting them since I was let out of Holiner. Each one tells a story. I've lost count, but there must be at least a quarter of a million dollars in this cabinet alone."

Ben felt a lump in his throat, not from Charles passively insulting him or boasting of the insane price tag of the booze, but from his mentioning that place.

Holiner.

Perhaps it was the sparking of painful memories. Perhaps it was guilt. "How long were you in there, a hundred years?" Ben asked with an awkward laugh.

"Twenty-two years, but no less than a hundred, or so it felt." Charles searched the shelves for the perfect spirit to share. He reached into the back of his collection and brought out a dusty, amber bottle. "Here it is. How's does this suit your taste?" He handed the bottle to his old friend.

"Sure, I love a good wine as much as anyone. Grape juice with a kick."

"It's cognac. I've been saving it for our inevitable reunion."

Ben read the label. "Cognac Salignac. Sounds like something a duke would drink. I bet it's worth a small fortune, eh?"

"A small fortune of $12.99," Charles said. "At least, that was the price I paid back then. It was the first thing I bought when they let me out of Holiner. They gave me a set of clothes, a bus ride to town, and fifty dollars, the first thirteen of which went to our commemorative cognac."

"I'm touched," Ben said, uneasy from the fact that he was the first thing on Charles's mind when he rejoined the world.

"I bought it just for you. Despite the discount price, it's my most prized possession."

The last thing Ben wanted to talk about was their time at Holiner. He was afraid of bringing up something dangerous, delicate, something that would erase their decades apart. If absence can make the heart grow fonder, if being out of sight means being out of mind, Ben figured that their sudden reunion might prove the opposite and rip everything to shreds.

On a polished walnut table at the base of the cabinet, Charles set down two elegant, gold-rimmed goblets, placing the bottle of cheap cognac between them. He waved his hand, promptly sending one of his men out of the room. Ben felt relieved to see one less goon with them and drooled at the thought of the liquor being served. He imagined it trickling across his tongue, then pouring down his gullet. Over the years, he'd grown an unfortunate affinity to such indulgences.

"It must be hard to have limited freedom," Charles said. "Really, it's another way of saying you have no freedom. You made it out of

Holly, free as a bird, but a hunted one, doomed to be chased by the law for the rest of your life. I recently read about a 90-year-old man who was caught and tossed back in a 6x8 cell after escaping when he was 22. The media can be a powerful tool. I'd be nervous if I were in your shoes."

"You gonna turn me in, Charlie?" Ben asked, keeping up his jovial facade. "Is that why I'm here? Last I heard, there's still a hefty bounty on my head." To his surprise, his stoic friend laughed. "I figure if anyone's ever gonna claim that payday, might as well be you, eh?"

"Ben Stoll," Charles said, his laugh fading with a sigh. "Clearly, you haven't changed at all."

"Is that a good thing?"

"You always did fail to see things through another man's eyes. Take a look around. Hefty bounty? Do I look as though I need help with finances?"

"Even rich men are motivated by money," Ben said sharply. "Especially rich men."

"The chandelier above you cost more than the reward for your capture tenfold, and I have one in every room. No, my friend, I actually sent for you so that I may reunite us before the authorities become skillful. Stranger things have happened."

"Then what's for me to be nervous about?" Ben asked in his raspy voice of rugged confidence. "I made it this far, more than twenty-five years, and I can make it to the end."

"The end," Charles said with a grin. "Yes, you just might reach the end, wherever or whatever that is. You were always the lucky one."

The silent guard returned with a corkscrew, linen napkins, and a small, fine wooden box that looked as if it were designed for a wristwatch. Charles plunged the screw into the cognac, pausing in reflection of what he'd just said. "But to live the way you do, always dirty, always looking over your shoulder, no one knowing who you really are... it's beneath you. When we were lads, everyone knew who Bennie and Charlie were."

"Hell yeah, they did!" Ben said, smiling with pride. "Everyone who knew what was good for 'em!"

"But things change, I suppose. I'm much older now. My name still has weight, just in different circles. I haven't been called 'Charlie' for decades, not until you walked in the room just now."

"'Charles Goldwine,' is it now?" Ben smirked. "No more Charlie Gold? No more Charlie Parlay?"

"Only on your lips."

Ben looked about the room, at the opulence surrounding him. "Tell me Charlie, Charles The Businessman, what kind of money buys this life? Level with me, is all this stuff hot or clean?"

"A fine blend of both. I enjoy balancing the two. It keeps me on my toes, as I'm sure you're on yours."

"I gotta be," Ben said, waiting for the cognac.

"I remember you were quite alert the day of the breakout." Charles poured the liquor into his goblet, preparing to fill his friend's as well.

Ben placed a hand over his glass as the bottle tilted. The tension in the air was undeniable, and he wanted to clear it before the drink he so desperately craved. "What do you mean, Charlie? Is there something you want to get off your chest?"

"I suppose you could say that." Charles looked at his suspicious friend and flashed him a reassuring smile. "Don't worry, we'll get to it."

"Please do." Ben relaxed his hand, allowing Charles to fill his goblet. He scrutinized the stream of amber spirit for a moment, as if to find something floating within. "Share it with me. Come on, Charlie, you never could fool me."

Charles set down the $12.99 bottle, sat back in his leather chair, and raised his goblet to the light of the chandelier. "It certainly does sound odd hearing 'Charlie'. No one's called me that since... well, since Holiner."

"That tears it!" Ben said, his raised voice killing the thick tension. The bodyguards shifted their stance, ready for a fight. Ben knew they'd be on him quick and that he couldn't handle two meathead thugs like he used to. "You got a chip on your shoulder about our days in the joint! I ain't touching that booze 'till we settle this."

"Afraid of a simple drink between friends?" Charles asked. "Is that what's become of you? A wild animal who trusts no one?"

"I've always been able to drop your ass! It was true the day I took you off the streets, and it's true today!"

"I was barely nineteen then," Charles said, holding his drink up to the room light. "I'm much older now, and I have these able men working for me. Be assured, at the blink of an eye, any of them can 'drop your ass' with a bullet before your next breath, whether it be the two in this room or the others out in the hall. However, that will not happen."

"Don't count this old man out," Ben said, his face red with fury. "I got the skin of a rhino after what life's dealt me! That's something you and your high society assholes can never understand!"

"You're a survivor."

"You're goddamn right!" Ben looked at the floor, struggling to calm himself. He felt the silence that stood between them teetering on the edge, and he feared the fall. "Look, I'm gonna tell ya, things haven't been good. I'm a bum. I'll say it out loud, I'm nobody no more, just a ghost counting the days. You should be happy you didn't bust out back when I did. Feel lucky that The Man made you stick to your years inside. You know you're far better off than I'll ever be."

Charles raised his glass to take a drink, pausing just as the rim was near his lips. "You are right about some things, Ben. There is a chip on my shoulder, a great big chip. It does regard Holiner State Penitentiary. But it wasn't about our days inside, rather one particular day."

"The breakout."

"Drink your cognac."

"After you," Ben said, smiling, lowering into a chair opposite his host. "Seems like you're waiting for me, but it'd be rude for a guest to take the first sip before the lord of the manor."

"Please, give me some dignity," Charles said. "You can smell it, swish it in your mouth. I promise, I won't take offense."

"I taught you everything, Charlie, those years on the grift before we were shoved into Holly. We both know poison don't always have a taste or stink. Now are you gonna drink first or is there gonna be an ugly scene? I don't give a shit if you got two guys or ten ready to strong-arm me."

Charles stared down his guest like a poker player sizing up his opponent. "You asked me to share my history with you. First, let's share this drink. Here's to our enduring friendship." Charles raised his goblet to the light and swirled the cheap liquor-store cognac as if it were rare Burgundy. He put the glass to his lips and slowly took in the spirit, swishing it in his mouth, swallowing it quickly. "The most sensuous poison I've ever tasted. Quite robust."

Ben felt satisfied and engulfed his entire cognac in one tilt of his glass. Charles filled both their goblets again, and they shared another drink in tense silence. Though Charles drank along with him, Ben couldn't shake the feeling that he was making a grave mistake, a feeling so strong that he knew it to be true. "What have you done to me?" he asked, his voice a timid whisper.

Charles grinned. "As you said, I've never been able to fool you. Until now."

Ben dropped his goblet to the floor, the padded rug keeping it intact.

"You did teach me a lot of things," Charles said, "how to steal, how to lie, how to bleach guilt. But I've learned a few tricks since then." He noticed doubt in his friend's face. "Your goblet was lined with the poison, behind the gold rim."

"You son of a bitch," Ben said, ready to stomp his taunting goblet on the floor. "I should've known you'd be trouble. When your goons grabbed me, told me who wanted to see me, I should've took off running. You want revenge? For what? You blame me for making you a crook? I didn't force you to do those jobs with me. And before we were nabbed, you didn't have no problems robbin' folks. You blame me for your stretch in the joint? Face it, I busted out and you didn't. Tough shit, pal. It's not my fault you didn't have the balls to make it."

Charles corked the bottle, rose from his chair, and returned it to the cabinet like a souvenir. Hearing his old partner's fearful rant, he beamed with confidence, the same confidence that used to belong to Ben when they were in the same gang, back when they were plotting heists and creating confidence scams, back when they shared the same prison sentence at Holiner. A new man was at the wheel now, and it was a first for Ben. He'd never been scared like this before.

"So what's this stuff, Charlie? Am I gonna have the hiccups till Christmas? Am I gonna itch for the next six months? Maybe I'll pass out and wake up on the front steps of the 15th Precinct?"

Charles cupped his hands in his lap, speaking with an eerily calm demeanor. "Your insides will slowly melt like candles in a boiler room, as will your skin. Along the way, your eyesight will fade, your hearing, your sense of touch. By then, however, your brain's synapses will have become broth, so you won't feel much. The climactic finale to this retribution, of course, is your reunion with

The Almighty, assuming He accepts you into His kingdom and assuming He exists."

As he'd done all his life, Ben fought his fear with rage. "Fuck you and your bluff and your ten-cent words," Ben said. "I don't care how big your house is, you ain't nothing but a bitter, old, has-been crook throwing a tantrum, and you ain't never had the guts to take a man down." Despite his bold words, Ben realized the calculating manner in which his former partner and cellmate described his plight. Charles had never been the type to kill – that was always Ben's department – but now seemed to welcome the chance. Somehow, Ben knew the terror he felt was genuine.

Confirmation came when he felt a surge within his stomach. Something was indeed happening, doubling the fear overtaking him. "Name it," Ben said to his host as he clutched his stomach. "You win. You got me dead to rights. What is it you want?"

"You have no funds," Charles said, "or possessions of any kind. You have no identity, so I can't blackmail you, and you can't get a job to pay me money for the rest of your life. We both know you're too old to be of any use to my business and too wanted to be seen near me as my slave."

"There's gotta be something you want from me, you son of a bitch! You had this planned! Stop fucking around and get to it!"

Charles sat back in his deep leather chair and rested his legs on a footstool. He looked up at the chandelier. "Do you remember what we called the breakout?"

"What?" Ben said, confused by the sudden change in tone.

"Do you remember what the escape plan was called? It was most ingenious, I must commend you on that. You always were good with strategy, as foolhardy as it often was. We had a special name for the breakout."

"I don't know. I forgot. It was a long time ago." Ben clutched his aching stomach.

"How funny," Charles said, "because it's burned into my memory. We called it 'The Holy Corridor.' Looking back at the plan now, it was beautiful." He picked up the small wooden box from his desk and held it into the air. On cue, one of his guards approached him, took the box from his hand, and carried it out of the room.

"What was that?" Ben asked, afraid of the answer.

"You'll see in a moment." Charles drank the rest of his cognac and sat quietly in his chair.

"How long?" Ben asked with a groan. "How long before..."

"An hour, give or take."

Ben's striking pain spread throughout his body, the agony immeasurable. Some moments, it took all his effort just to remain standing as he felt a raw fear he'd never imagined. The pain and the thought of his innards melting tempted him to ask for a mercy killing, but even in his desperation he would deny Charles the satisfaction of watching him beg. "You ungrateful prick. I kept you alive on the street and protected you in the joint. Why would you do this to the one guy who had your back? How can you just sit there while I die? We were a team, you and me! Bennie and Charlie! Remember?"

"It was only a hundred feet long," Charles said as he pictured the past and ignored Ben's present torment. "Seemed much longer back then."

"What the hell are you talking about?" Ben screamed as he doubled over.

"The Holy Corridor. It was one-hundred feet long and twenty feet wide, yet it seemed like a vast warehouse." Charles spoke as if reliving the cursed day more for his guards than his victim. "A section of the power plant below the prison had water running underneath it."

"What the hell is this?" Ben said. The sharp pangs in his stomach clawed at him.

"The prison's power came from a nearby waterfall, and huge canals networked everywhere. Across one of them was Freedom. All we had to do was figure out a way across. *You* figured out a way, of course, the man with the plan." Charles excitedly pantomimed with his hands as he spoke. "We busted apart a rotted door with our boots and belts, then tied the splintered lumber to some utility piping for a makeshift bridge across the canal, only a couple of inches wide." Charles turned to face Ben. "I was no tightrope walker, and I feared the narrow structure was too weak, but you were certain it would hold us if we crossed one at a time."

"Enough!"

"Not nearly enough!" Charles turned to his guards. "The water below was alive with electricity. That was the Ben Stoll stroke of genius. To ensure we weren't followed, he cut the power tubes and tossed the exposed cables into the canal. Brilliant. Only desperate men would be able or willing to take the risk, not the guards earning their barely living wage. Finally, on the day of the breakout..."

"I know what happened!" Ben said.

Charles ignored him, continuing to speak to the room. "On the day of the breakout, we hopped onto the crude bridge and made our way down the corridor, crossing the baptizing waters. You made it across easy, always the athletic one, but I was not so sure of myself. I froze on the middle of the bridge, terrified of losing my balance and falling into the water to be deep-fried. I never made it across. Instead, I looked over to where you were and didn't see you. I imagined the guards beating the tar out of you. I even considered the possibility that a tower pig nailed you with his scoped rifle. It wasn't until weeks later, when I was rotting in solitary, that I learned you made it out and left me alone to fend for myself. The one guy who 'had my back' ended up turning his away."

Charles Goldwine stared at his former partner Ben Stoll, his brow turned inward, a wild look about him. Ben knew his deranged captor was capable of anything now.

"Listen to me," Ben said. "You're better off now. You made your sentence stick and now you've got clout. You told me to look around, now you look! This house, those clothes, you're big time, bigger than we ever were back in the day. Me, what do I got? I'm an invisible man, a stray dog, except to the cops. You said it yourself, I can't stay in one spot, can't get a job, can't tell people my name. I'm just an old grifter with bad knees, blurry eyes, and a crooked spine, sleeping in bushes by the highway. Ain't all that punishment enough for my sins? Why the hell would a man like you, a man who's got the world in the palm of his hand, want to mess with a skid like me? What could I have taken from you that was so bad?"

"Like I told you, Ben," Charles said. "I never made it across that bridge."

Charles lifted his shirt above his head, exposing his chest and back. The grotesque, discolored contortions and puffy labyrinths of dripping flesh were beyond disfigurement. From the neck down, Charles simply wasn't human. He looked as if he should have been screaming in pain, as if he should have been screaming constantly for the rest of his life. "My lower body is much worse, my legs almost unrecognizable. They barely fit in my pants."

"Jesus Christ," Ben muttered, backing away from the hideous sight.

"No, unfortunately, Jesus Christ wasn't there, but the canal was only so deep. My head and hands were above the surface, so they were spared, more or less. Doctors pumped me full of drugs that I depend on to this day. They had the audacity to call my survival no less than a miracle. Do I look like a miracle to you?"

Ben tried to convince himself that it was all a joke, that Charles was wearing a Halloween monster costume, but the more he stared at the pulpy figure of a man, the more he realized it couldn't be a trick. "I'm sorry Charlie, I... I didn't know."

"Of course not. You were too busy expanding the distance between the prison and yourself. So busy, in fact, that you let me fry, screaming out for anyone to remove me from the water. I must have cooked for nearly a minute, the diluted voltage not enough to kill me but enough to deny me passage. I waited to die, I hoped to die. Folks say I was lucky. On that, I disagree."

Charles took a cigar from his inside pocket and lit it. He reclined in his chair, enjoying the smoke. "But on to matters at hand. I have a gift for you."

Two of Charles's guards walked to Ben's side, gesturing for him to rise and follow them. They escorted him to a set of ornate double doors that stood near the liquor cabinet, opposite the exit.

"Open the doors," Charles said, as if it were a suggestion rather than a command.

Ben's first reaction was to refuse to cooperate. A sudden burst in his chest, followed by deep pains in his gut, reminded him of his disadvantage. "I didn't want this, Charlie. I never wished this on you."

"When you've invested in revenge for as long as I have, you forget the reasoning behind things. You replace justified retribution with symbolism. Call this a symbol, of our renewed friendship and of my quelled anguish."

Ben hoped for the worst to pass quickly and opened the doors before him. The silence that passed through the doorway was dominant, and Ben saw nothing inside at first. It was dark to a point where all light seemed to die. A moment later, dim lamps came on, exposing a devilish design.

"Behold, The Holy Corridor," Charles said. "An exact replica, true in every detail to the original. Every spot of mildew, every mosquito, every drop of tainted water. I've even had a sound system installed to help recreate the blazing roars of the machinery back at Holly. Doesn't this bring it all back, friend?"

Ben's pains were becoming more possessive, and he would normally have dropped to the floor by that point. He knew, however, that if he were to live, he needed to bite the bullet and play out whatever mad game Charles had created.

The obsession behind Charles's replica was frightening. Just as he said, the recreation of the breakout was perfect. Ben could tell that it must have taken months, perhaps years, to build something so immense, so detailed.

"What would you have me do, Charlie?"

"You know what to do," Charles said. "Make it to freedom, just like you did decades ago, freedom now being the cure for your ailment, which you'll find on the other end of that bridge."

The corridor's pipe bridge looked just as flimsy as the original, made of various sized wooden boards and pipes bound together in a hurry. At the end of the corridor, a small table waited with the fine wooden box on it. From its long, narrow shape, Ben knew that was indeed his freedom – a syringe full of it.

"Let me know if there's anything missing," Charles said.

"Dogs," Ben said, hoping it would buy him more time. "There was a pack of guard dogs at the end. They attacked me the second I hopped off the pipe bridge."

"Oh, they're present. As I recall, they didn't pounce on you, revealing themselves, until you were inches away from escape. Now if you'll step onto the piping, we can get this underway. The sooner you start, the sooner you finish, and we can resume our friendship again."

Ben carefully stepped onto the bridge, feeling it wobble with the slightest touch. "I tell you one thing, Charlie," he said. "Whether or not I make it past this, you can take our friendship and shove it back into the hell hole you crawled out of."

"In that case, you are nothing but entertainment," Charles said with a demented scowl. "My only effort will be to enjoy another cognac while I watch you die, and my sole regret is that I'll only get to witness it once. You will most likely die, of course. The one alteration I made to this replica is an increase in voltage. This polluted water is much more fierce than that of Holiner's, and I suspect it will eliminate any chance of survival should you fall in."

Ben took a few quick steps across the bridge, scooting along the way he did when he was younger, no less desperate. "What happens after I make it?" he said, yelling over the simulated machinery, concentrating on his feet.

"If you make it, including past the dogs, my men will shut off the power. You can then safely join me on this side, wading through the dormant water in a victory dance, as much as your bad knees can allow."

Ben barely heard his captor as he balanced himself, moving down the spindly bridge with careful pace. For what seemed like hours, the sounds of machinery blared into his head, accompanied by a rain of mosquitos peppering his face and arms. He was going to make it, he could feel it. The box was within clear sight, only twenty feet more to go.

Suddenly, an enormous blast of scorching hot air shot out of one of the machine walls, making the entire corridor rumble as if a freight train passed overhead. The makeshift bridge shook, and Ben flailed his arms wildly, trying to recapture balance. In the distance, he could hear Charles laughing into his cognac, waiting for the finale of his grand production.

About to plummet into the scathing river, Ben blindly leaped for the ledge ahead of him. His fingers miraculously caught the wet concrete, and he dangled inches from the deadly water. It made a crackling sound that sent fear through him, mentally pulling him downward like a great magnet.

Lynn Harrod

Straining to climb out of the canal, he felt sharp stabs on his hands. The drowning thunder of dogs barking was all around him. He wearily hung onto the ledge, watching hordes of beasts tear at his flesh.

"Wonderful, aren't they?" Charles said, his voice now bellowing over the sound system. "I wager any of these handsome fellows could rip a Holiner dog to shreds. Where were they when we needed them?"

Ben shoved at the dogs, holding onto the ledge with one arm. His muscles burning and ripping apart, he made his way up to level ground. The dogs made it nearly impossible to get to his feet.

"I call them my Little Bennies," Charles said, "because they're the coldest, most heartless bastards I could find."

Ben swung his arms violently, grabbing at his dozen attackers. There was no way to hurt them in such large numbers and nothing to hurt them with. Seeing one of the dogs dangerously close to the ledge gave him a thought.

He lunged at a dense group of dogs, sending them tumbling into the deadly water. He clutched another by the collar, the dog ripping into his forearms, and hurled it into the canal. Another four dogs pinned him down. He spun on his back and kicked them over the edge, one by one, until there were no killers left sharing his floor. The beasts were instantly destroyed by the unimaginable intensity of the voltage. Their bodies bled from every pore, twisting into bizarre contortions as they cried. Ben felt queasy from the sight, remembering it was to be his fate.

He turned to the small table, eye-level with the wooden box. He slid it off its table and held it high above his head, blood dripping from countless bites on his arms and torso.

"I've got your box!" Ben said, screaming down the corridor at Charles. "I've got your fucking box!" He fell to his knees to keep from stumbling over the edge, the blood loss and poison taking their toll.

Charles sat in his chair, quiet, emotionless. He revealed a remote control from his pocket and used it to shut off the power to the corridor. The storm of sound effects stopped, throwing the scene into a eerie silence. "Good man," he said, his voice echoing off the steel walls. "You may return now."

"How do I know the power is really off?" Ben asked, catching his breath.

Charles nodded to one of his guards. The dark-suited man rolled up his sleeve and held his hand under the water's surface without harm. Seeing this, Ben jumped into the canal and headed back to his host's parlor, drudging through the bloody remains of the pack of dogs.

"Congratulations," Charles said as Ben climbed out of the canal. "The main goal was to kill you, but part of me is happy you've made it out. I don't care how wealthy a man is, a show like this just can't be bought."

"No it can't," Ben said, panting, "but now your sick show's over." He opened the wooden box in his hands, expecting to see the syringe that would save his life. Instead, he found a silver fork and steak knife. "What the hell is this?"

"Freedom, as I promised."

"What is this, a hoax? Am I really dying, Charlie?"

"Yes, you most certainly are dying. In no way did I arrange all this for nothing. In fact, the clock gives you only fifteen minutes before the poison kicks in beyond reversal. That's just an estimate, of course."

"You bastard." Ben readied to tackle Charles, but was halted by a deep pain in his stomach. He could feel his insides burning. The two guards in the room held their guns close as he huddled into a ball, groaning, clutching his gut.

"Put the guns away," Charles said to his servants. "The man is in no shape to..."

A guard fell to the floor as Ben jammed the steak knife in his side. In a blur, he stabbed at the man again and again, making sure he was out of the picture. He thrust his foot at the other guard as he reached for his gun. Another second later, Ben was on him, slashing, screaming.

The guards died violently, and a suddenly scared Charles called out for the others in the hall. Ben took the guns from the bloody floor and fired two-handed mercilessly at the incoming guards, killing them in a slaughter before they knew what was happening.

When the gunfire stopped, Charles Goldwine and Benjamin Stoll were alone. To Ben's dismay, Charles had his own gun now, pointed straight at Ben's head.

"I've never used this before," Charles said about his antique pistol, grasping for control. "The man I purchased it from assures me that no one has. Original condition. Flawless. It would be a shame for me to break the chain, but it would be an honor for you to be the first to fall to it."

"Go ahead and pull the trigger," Ben said, exhausted. "See if it gets you what you wanted. I've had enough of your fool bluster."

"Don't you want to know where the serum is? I'd love for you to have..."

Without a word, Ben raised his gun and fired, plugging Charles in the stomach, sending him to his knees. His gun and goblet tumbled from his hands.

"You never were the killing kind," Ben said, struggling to breathe, "least not when the chips were down and you were face-to-face with a man."

Charles sat on the floor against the side of his chair, patiently awaiting his end. After an initial expression of searing pain, an odd smile formed on his face, trickling blood from its corners. "I've received more than I bargained for, but I got what I wanted. I don't think I'd ever have the courage to finish this miserable existence myself. You have my gratitude, Ben, my deepest gratitude."

Ben's body was failing fast, his vision fading and his skin freezing. He rested his gun's barrel against Charles's forehead. "Where's the serum?" he asked. "If there is one, I'd like to have it now."

Charles coughed blood, making it difficult to speak. "You may fire if you wish, but I won't deprive you of your life, old friend. I'm a man of my word, always have been."

"So where is it? Where the syringe that was in this box?"

"Yes, I believe there was a syringe at first," Charles said, looking up at his chandelier. "I wanted to ensure you a hearty last meal in the event you didn't discover the serum in time. So I took the liberty of injecting it into one of the late Bennies. It coursed through his bloodstream. I hope your search is fruitful, as I would guess you only have a few minutes left, a few more than myself."

On that final word, Charles succumbed to his wound, sliding down the side of his leather chair until he laid lifeless on the floor.

Ben listened for breathing, but there was none. Confused, on the brink of collapse, he replayed his former partner's strange last words. He looked back at The Holy Corridor, the canal filled with a dozen dead dogs, and realized in horror what he was about to do.

Holding the wooden box in his hand, he admired the beauty of the elegant, silver knife and fork, and walked back to the corridor's still, baptizing water.

Rapeseed

"Are you bleeding?"

Grace opened her eyes to a serene meadow with cranes standing in a pond, country folk lying on the grass around an ancient oak, and a man in silhouette standing against the tree, his arms outstretched. As her vision came into focus, and she felt her back ache against the cold cement floor, she realized she was looking at a painting on the ceiling.

"Grace!"

She recognized Josie's voice as it drifted across the basement toward her, the room's details shifting, blurry, as she slowly woke to her friend's urgent tone.

"Are you bleeding?" Josie asked again, desperate. "Is that blood yours? Grace, you okay?"

Grace pushed herself upright, her long red hair peeling off the sticky floor. To her horror, she realized the tacky feeling of the cement came from laying in a thin pool of blood. She didn't know how long she'd been there, but it was long enough that the blood started to clot, fusing her to the floor. Grace instinctively kept calm in response to her friend who sounded ready to lose her mind.

"Is that your blood?" Josie asked again, her voice cracking and spiraling with her emotions. "Why won't you answer me?"

"Not mine," Grace said, feeling about her body. As she slid her hands around her head, arms, and torso, pieces of her memory floated to her. The forming scene startled her but still felt like a dream. "You hurt?"

"No. You?"

"Not bad, just cuts and scrapes." Grace's relief at being relatively unharmed shattered upon realizing that she'd been laying in *someone else's* blood. Though not fresh, it still looked shiny, felt sticky, which meant someone else had laid there recently. That poor soul had surely been restrained with the same heavy chains that now weighed down her arms.

Grace looked around the basement – Josie to her left, Carmen to her right, and a stairwell across the room that climbed into darkness. She stretched her body as far as her twin chains would allow, barely getting her arms at full length.

Grace wiped away the dried blood caked on the side of her face. Moving her arms the slightest inch sent a sting through her from the pinching edges of her shackles. After enduring the initial, frightening rush of remembering her plight, her vision became foggy. That damned drug still flowed through her veins. She saw that Josie's wounds were like her own, minor cuts and bruises on her arms, only she had many more of them.

Josie didn't lay sprawled on the floor as Grace had. She stood chained to a crumbling stone wall, hands out like Jesus on the cross, unable to relax her legs without the agony of her wrists tearing apart from bearing her full weight. At least she was conscious, frantically searching the room with her eyes as if it were a sadistic puzzle to be solved.

Carmen appeared to be in the worst shape of the three. She hung unconscious, dangling from her chains, blood soaking her white designer afghan blouse.

"Carmen?" Grace said, her unspoken question clear.

"Still here," Josie said in an exhale, her way of saying their friend was alive. "She moved a minute ago."

Grace felt a chill as she took in their grim situation. With that seed oil in her brain, it was difficult to recall exactly how they ended up trapped in that basement. Merely forming a thought was painful, like a miniature hammer to the forehead.

"Do you remember anything?" Josie asked in a near-whisper.

Grace shook her head, still looking about the room.

"I pissed myself, Grace," Josie said, whining, the embarrassing confession tumbling out. "I think I'm going to puke. What the hell happened?"

"Let me think," Grace said, barely able to breathe, much less speak in any coherent manner. As she strained to recollect the evening, her vision cleared. She noticed the odd elegance of the room – ornate wood carvings along the walls, a tiled, painted ceiling, expressionist art hung high, and varnished hardwood that bordered the polished concrete. Such indulgent details seemed unusual for a basement that doubled as a dungeon. One doesn't normally obsess over the beauty of a room meant for a boiler, mops and brooms, bottles of bleach, and three abducted college girls. Aesthetics shouldn't matter unless, of course, the adorned basement served a greater purpose.

"Rich room," Grace said, muttering.

"Who gives a shit about..." Josie cut off her panicked reply when replayed her friend's comment a moment later. "Yes! He is rich!" She struggled to recall any further details.

"He?"

"The guy in the limo! I'm remembering now! Shit, I hope Carmen is still alive."

I hope Carmen is still alive.

The words were alarming to hear aloud.

Grace blew her red hair out of her face to take another look at her dozing friend. "Yeah, she's alive. I can see her breathing. But look at her shirt. It's soaked red. There's a puddle around her feet..."

"Jesus!" Josie screamed, silencing herself, shutting her eyes tight as if that would undo their ordeal, either heal her mutilated girlfriend or make her vanish from sight. She glanced at the stairwell out of the corner of her eye. It was the only way in or out of the basement, and she and Grace both knew that whoever they were trying to remember could walk down those steps at any moment. "Are you in shock? How can you be so calm?"

Grace ignored her friend as frenzied images sped through her mind, overlapping in confusion. The rave in the crowded warehouse... their boyfriends fighting with the disc jockey in some petty squabble... the police raiding the warehouse, arresting anyone too stoned or drunk to bolt... Josie and Carmen calling out to her amid the chaos... finding the busted seam in a corrugated metal wall... pulling back the metal to squeeze their bodies outside.

Perhaps it was shock, perhaps it was the drug, but Grace certainly appeared calm in their hopeless situation. She saw Josie falling apart and wanted only to console her, to keep her mind from running away. Grace assumed her calm stemmed from that longtime role as the the brash, fearless leader of the trio. "You said something about a limo?"

"Yeah, the limo!" Josie said, seeing that Grace couldn't yet recall the party's aftermath. "When they busted the rave, we broke out through that hole in the wall you made. We crawled out and ended up in the alley."

Grace hadn't found any hole. She made one by shoving the DJ's equipment cart against a split seam in the thin metal wall. With her two friends drunk and high, ready to faint or scream in the mass confusion as officers cuffed party-goers all around, she had to do something. "I remember the hole, and I remember us in the alley." Grace relived the chilling panic that swept over her when they burst from the loud, crowded warehouse, alive with colorful strobing lights and hordes of people fleeing in all directions, out into the silent, dark alley.

"We heard a car coming," Josie said, following her disjointed, returning memory. "We thought it was the cops, so we ran down the alley to a dead end. But it wasn't the cops, it was..."

"The limo," Grace recalled. "A black stretch Lincoln." She traced her chains to the busted bolts that came loose from the stone wall, which left her flat on the floor, unlike her companions. Though still restrained, she had more slack. She wiggled her arms and realized her thin wrists were loose within their shackles. "I think I can slip out of these!"

Grace winced as she painfully slid her left hand free. She quickly tried to free her other hand to no avail. Seeing a trash can full of brooms and garden tools in a corner by the stairwell, she reached as far as she could for something. Anything. Her chains rendered it hopeless.

"Wait, I'm closer," Josie said. "I think I can kick something with my feet..."

The girls fell silent when they heard the unseen door at the top of the stairs creak open, spilling light along the steps in a jagged line. Before Grace could form another thought, she saw Josie playing possum, feigning that her sedative still held. Grace quickly followed her example, shoving her free hand back into its shackle.

A weathered old man in a red night robe entered the basement, smiling at his three unconscious prizes. In his hand was a small white box. "What a mess you are, young lady," he said to Carmen, the one girl still genuinely unconscious. He approached her and carefully removed her blouse.

Grace could only imagine the hideous things he must have been doing to her friend. She heard Carmen's clothes being torn off, the snipping of scissors for the stubborn parts. Though Grace dreaded opening her eyes for fear of being next, she peered through her disorientation, amazed by what she saw.

The old man tended to Carmen's wounds with a first aid kit, carefully dressing what looked like irreparable damage. "I will not forgive myself for letting this happen," he said to her as if she were awake. "The body and mind are two halves. They must both be in polished health." He wrapped her arms in gauze and repeated himself. "The body and mind are two halves. They must both be in polished health."

The old man's words flung open a door in Grace's foggy memory, suddenly purging the cloaking drug from her entirely. Whereas she could barely picture the limousine before, she could remember it in vivid detail now.

"I'm sorry about the rough treatment," the old man had said earlier in the limousine as they sped through the city, enshrouded in darkness as if he were a living shadow.

The three girls were all weak, unable to move as they lay in a pile in front of him on the grand vehicle's floor. The struggle, and the drug that was injected into them promptly thereafter, made the old man seem different then.

Grace remembered thinking that only two hours before, they were sitting together in Mr. Simonian's Psychology class, bored from the lecture, looking forward to a wild night out at a secret rave that Carmen had heard about. Through her fear, Grace wondered at how much had changed in such a short time. Her self-defense classes warned her about the swiftness of an opportunistic predator.

The old man's voice was markedly deeper then, echoing and distorting like a warped record being played too slow. His kind eyes, which was all they could see of him, betrayed his determined will to get these young girls to submit.

Passed out and beaten bloody in the back of that limo – the result of attempting to defy the man's wrath – Carmen would remember none of this. More drunk than brave, she put up a fiercer fight than her two companions and therefore was the first to feel the brunt of the disturbed man's sudden aggression.

"Your friend forced me to take more violent actions in getting her to enter the car. She's quite a force when she allows herself to be." From their viewpoint, the girls saw a living shadow speak, its expressions shown only through kind, glowing white eyes staring at them. "But please don't alarm yourselves. I promise to mend her wounds."

"Where... we going?" Grace asked, weak and immobile, the words stumbling from her lips. "What... have you done?"

"Let us out of here... you freak," Josie muttered in a blank tone, dazed and fixed on their captor.

"We're almost there, be patient," he said. "The trip will seem all the more brief for you. The rapeseed will take you into dream shortly."

"What is this?" Grace murmured, frantically feeling the spot on her arm where a syringe fed her the drug moments before. She had only to hear the utterance of the word "rape" to find herself gripped by paralyzing fear.

"It's an Asian drug," her captor said, "made from the oil extract of the rapeseed. I assure you, it has nothing to do with the act of rape, though I suppose it could assist such a vile act. It's quite a morbid name for such an efficient, harmless sedative. It will relieve you for an hour. In no way do I want any harm to come to you young ladies yet."

Yet.

The word punctuated their peril. Grace and Josie were left to imagine what that meant, and their host could somehow hear their many unspoken questions clearly. He seemed to have a bizarre sympathy for his victims, despite being the source of their pain.

"No matter how many times I've taken prey, I always feel for them. It's hypocritical, considering how often I feed. Unfortunately, I can't blindly buy my meat from the market like most ignorant fools who claim to feel emotion for food animals. I have to hunt them personally. It makes one wonder how many people would continue to eat meat if forced to hunt and kill their dinners, as in the old ways. I wager there would be many more vegans in the world." He smiled upon that reflection.

Grace knew exactly what this man was saying. She cried silently as an insane fear diluted with a frightening acceptance washed over her. Josie merely slipped into a dream, succumbing to the drug.

"Don't give me tears," he said with pity. "I don't want this any more than you do, believe me. I don't take prey nearly as much as I should, only hunting once a month because it pains me so. To spare others such misery, I starve myself between the nights I venture out to hunt."

"Then... let us go," Grace said on the edge of surrendering to the seed oil.

"I almost wish you would kill me," he said. "It would save us both, ending my torment. Killing me is quite possible, despite what storybooks tell you. However, I have become adept at catching prey, especially youth. Call it a blessing. Call it a curse."

He's a vampire, Grace thought in despair. *More like he's a fucking psycho obsessed with vampires, obsessed with Anne Rice novels, seen too many movies.*

"I'm no vampire."

Did I say that out loud?

"And I don't know anyone named Anne."

Yes, I must have.

"Don't trouble yourself trying to study me," the dark man said. "What I am has no label. But if you need one, I am called Dridyn. Like the mythical vampire, I need blood to nourish me. But unlike my fictional counterpart, I feast on the entire being of my prey, body and mind. A cup of your O-Negative simply wouldn't suffice."

Body and mind, Grace repeated in her head, unsure if the words remained in her thoughts. She could no longer tell, and she couldn't keep her eyes open much longer.

"I literally consume the whole of my prey. It adds to my existence to absorb another's. It enriches me, adding to me in ways I cannot sufficiently explain, a vicious, never-ending circle. The world continues to over-populate with weak, unsuspecting prey for me, while my body thrives and hunger grows with every soul I take. The universe does not revolve equally around its animals, I'm sad to say, even though I am at the advantage. But as conflicted as I often feel, I never release prey once I take it. It would be cruel on my part not to take the responsibility for a kill. A hunter should eat the deer he fells so that its death is not without purpose. As tempted as I may be, Dridyn can never release prey. Instead, the prey becomes part of me, lives on through my being."

Grace feebly reached out to the shadow man, feeling only an intense heat.

"Part of the role of the rapeseed is to help ease any guilt I may feel," he said. "As frightened as you may be, the seed oil is actually 'numbing' your fear a great deal. It makes me feel better about taking you, makes me feel like a considerate hunter. Fear poisons the meat more than the oil ever could. That's true of all food animals."

His words provided no solace. Though Grace could feel the cursed oil doing its job as Dridyn said, it instilled her with terror. In their pile, Grace felt streams of blood trickling onto her from Carmen's frail body above, barely alive. She worried about her friend, knowing well that they all shared the same fate.

Her captor once again read her face, or perhaps her mind.

"As I promised, I will tend to her wounds before I begin the evening. I need my prey to be whole. The body and mind are two halves. They both must be in polished health."

The last thing Grace saw before she drifted to sleep were her captor's sad, glowing eyes, looking down at her in mourning.

* * *

Watching the old man in red bandage Carmen in the basement made everything clear, though he seemed so different in the light of the underground room. As he described, he apparently needed them "whole" before feeding on them. This would buy them some small amount of time, she thought, fearing he could truly read her thoughts.

Lynn Harrod

"All finished with you," he said to Carmen's sleeping face. He gently laid her head against the wall, draping her long black hair down her shoulders as he shut the first aid kit and headed up the stairs. "When I return, I'll prepare you all for the evening."

A moment later, the upstairs door was closed again, the stairwell returning to darkness.

"I remember now!" Josie quickly said, trying desperately to free herself without making noise.

"I remember everything, too, Josie. Forget the chains, kick me that broom! Hurry!"

Josie kicked off her heels and stretched her ballet legs painfully, barely reaching a broom in the corner, knocking it to the ground from where it leaned against the stone wall. With her toes firmly gripping her dangling shoe, she slid the broom across the hardwood floor to her friend, who snatched it with her once-again free hand.

Using her hand and one of her feet, Grace strained to snap off the end of the old broom. The brittle handle broke in a splintered shatter of wood, creating a sharp weapon, a makeshift wooden stake fit for any storybook vampire. Remembering what he'd said in the limo, she hoped his confidence was high and blinding, and that some myths had truth to them.

Hiding the broken end of the handle behind her, she tossed the rest of the broom back to the shadowed, far corner. Her heart was near explosion as she thought of what she must do when the old man eventually returned for them. Through fear and nausea, she hoped she'd be first on his evening's list. Her stake would be worthless to her friends if he took one of them first. She could only reach so far.

In a stream of light from the stairwell, the old man in red returned to the basement. This time, a very wide awake Grace greeted him. Her pulse racing, she almost seemed eager.

"I see that you've opened your eyes this time," he said to her with a smile. It took Grace unaware that he knew she lay awake before. "Don't be shocked, young lady. The seed oil only lasts about an hour. I knew you were conscious. I simply didn't need to address you then."

Just a little closer, Grace thought, the splintered stake tucked into her pants behind her. Though her arms were both in shackles again, she prepared to free her left hand with deadly speed.

Instead of approaching her, however, he walked to the unconscious Carmen, examining her bandages. "Good, you're doing fine. You'll need more time to rest, so you'll be last." He rubbed her thick black hair in his palm. "Mexican with a hint of Portuguese, I'd guess." He walked across the room to Josie, who had also given up playing possum, her eyes fluttering open in a daze. "Irish, I'd say. Quite a flavor to you, so it has led me to believe. This will be a first."

Finally, after sizing up Josie for a minute, he walked to the awaiting Grace.

"What are you going to do now?" she asked him, hoping he would inch closer to her.

"You are truly pitiable, I sincerely mean that. I'm tempted to let you go off to your fathers, they're probably sweating nightmares now."

"Why don't you?" Grace persisted. "Why don't you just let us go?"

"I'm tempted," the old man said. "I'm always tempted. And I think this time... perhaps..." He paused in thought for a moment, removing a small black box from his robe pocket as he approached Grace.

Grace mustered what little strength she had left and swung her legs up and around her captor. She clutched him helpless just long enough to remove her left hand from its shackle, unsheathe her

Lynn Harrod

crude weapon, and thrust it into the old man's chest in a bloody pulp. He clutched the embedded stake and reeled back, tumbling onto the floor across the room.

Amazing, she thought, how easy it was to kill when her life hung before her. She experienced no remorse, instead sat fascinated by how this immortal creature's skin was almost like wet paper as she stabbed him solid and deep.

The old man stumbled to the floor in agony, dropping the black box. As the box broke open, three silver keys popped out and clattered onto the floor. He could only watch them tumble away as he felt his life running from him.

Grace immediately knew what those keys were for.

She grew withdrawn in a stupefying awe, stuttering as she spoke. "You were going to... oh no... no..."

"For the first time, I believe I was going to give in to temptation." The old man grunted, startled by how fast he was fading. "After years of preparing innocent ladies for the evening, my guilt caught up with me at last."

Josie tried to reach the old man, reach the keys across the floor, but couldn't come anywhere near them. Grace knew she would have no better luck.

"But you said Dridyn never releases prey!" Grace yelled in disbelief, trying to justify her killing him. "Dridyn never lets prey go, no matter how tempted!"

The old man looked up at the young girl with his sad eyes before falling to his wound. Sorrowed by the girls' fate, he strained to speak. "Thank you for freeing me," he said, mumbling. "Remember me. I am Petros... I long served the dark master with loyalty..."

"Petros!" Grace yelled, realizing her grave mistake. "The keys!"

"My debt... is now paid."

Eyes still open, the old man suddenly lay still and silent on the polished concrete floor, the broken broomstick impaled through his stomach, up into his heart.

In an instant, it all seemed clear. Grace desperately tugged at her chain for slack, trying to retrieve the stake from the old man's chest only a few feet away from her grasp. It was a pointless effort. Josie didn't share her friend's revelation, but she would know soon enough.

The stairwell grew dark again. In its doorway stood a shadowy figure with glowing white eyes. It paused as it saw its longtime servant dead on the floor and made a deep, strange groan that sounded like sorrow. This grief for its servant would only deaden any lingering remorse and fuel its building ferocity.

The tall living shadow descended the stairs and tended to his guests, beginning its long evening meal.

Lynn Harrod

Personal Devil

John Callender enjoyed the finest wine $3.99 could offer, a blend of Cabernet Sauvignon, Merlot, a bit of Syrah, and a slew of sweeteners and other additives, all held in its Central California bottle with a simple screw-top cap.

He sipped his cheap table wine while kneeling on the port side of his sixty-five-foot Seigneur de la Mer houseboat, sanding its cherry oak deck by hand. His detached garage was more than enough to hold his majestic boat, along with his Ferrari, Lotus, and Corvette. He worked the deck while listening to Bessie Smith, her crooning voice filling the garage as she sang blues classics from a boom box sitting on the bow.

Athletic and handsome for a man of 55, John's friends affectionately called him the "Silver Fox" of North End, the upscale suburban neighborhood known for its pristine households of disposable income. He checked the time on his black-and-silver Submariner wristwatch, the tenth time he glanced at it in as many minutes. Looking up from his timepiece, he flinched upon seeing his twelve-year-old daughter Kayla bounding in, a wide smile across her freckled face.

"Dad! You coming?"

"Kayla!" John said, sitting bolt upright. He slid off the sanding pads strapped to his palms, trying not to appear startled. "You gotta knock before you enter, honey. I might've had a sander running. It's dangerous to sneak up on someone with power tools."

"But you aren't using power tools," Kayla said, confused.

"I might've been. I almost was."

"But if you were, you wouldn't have heard me knock."

"No more 'but, but.' Don't argue with me, Kayla."

Kayla's energy sapped, she simply stood there looking up at her father on the Seigneur. "Sorry, Dad, I mean... I heard nothing but the music."

"Maybe I was about to turn on a drill?" John calmed himself and checked the time again. "Forget it. What's up?"

"We're starting. Restarting, actually."

Through a window – the only one of ten with its blinds raised – John could see his perfect family in his perfect home. His wife sat in a recliner, holding their new baby girl while his teenage son worked a pan of Jiffy Pop over the stove. Beyond them, John Wayne stood tall on a 98-inch TV mounted to the wall. The Hollywood legend seemed life-size as he walked through a small 1870s Oklahoma town, an eyepatch covering his left eye.

"*True Grit,*" John said. "Excellent choice."

"It was my turn to pick. I picked it for you."

The 1969 classic was John's favorite movie. Everyone knew his love for the film and his famous, absurd impression of its protagonist, Rooster Cogburn. For that reason alone, it was Kayla's favorite movie as well.

"What do you mean 'restarting'?"

"We got through the first scene," Kayla said, "but we're starting it over because Brenden was on the phone."

"That 'Larissa' girl again?" John and his daughter shared a laugh. For very different reasons, the notion that Brenden Callender was courting a young girl amused them. Interest in the opposite sex was still "pointless and illogical" to him only a year prior, as it still was to Kayla.

"What's with the blinds on the windows?" Kayla asked. "I don't think we've ever used 'em."

"The plan was to keep you all from seeing the boat before it's finished. I'm adding a lot of stuff. I wanted it to be a surprise."

"I guess I ruined that," Kayla said.

"And I guess I need to lock the door while I'm working in here."

"So, you coming?"

"You go," John said. "I need to work on this. I want to finish so we can take her out on the lake this weekend. Trout don't catch themselves."

"Is Uncle James gonna be there?" Kayla asked with a grin. "Or are you afraid he's gonna out-fish you like he always does?"

"He always out-fishes me because he always cheats," John said.

"Nah, he doesn't need to cheat. He uses my Good Luck Lure."

"Your what?"

"My Good Luck Lure," the girl said. "I made it for him last summer. Mom lost an earring and didn't want the other one anymore, so I made a fishing lure out of it. Uncle James says trout can't resist it!"

"You still call him 'uncle'?" John said, not hearing anything else she said. John never appreciated how his children referred to his business partner as "Uncle James," though they'd known him their entire lives. It pecked at his mind as he went back to sanding the deck.

"Leave it, Dad," Kayla said. "I can help you tomorrow."

John paused, feigning uncertainty, pretending that he was considering the offer. He shrugged and shook his head.

"Or... I can help you now. I mean, I've seen the movie before."

"And deprive you of your ninth time?" John said. He forced a smile. "It's fine. I'm expecting some business calls. Might as well work on the boat while I talk."

"Mom's right. You work too hard."

"Linda Callender thinks I work too hard?" John said with a laugh. "Can I get that in writing?"

"Why don't you call Uncle James? He knows all about boats."

John waved away the notion. He checked the time on his watch again.

Shit.

"Hey, go inside," John said. "Somebody has to explain the plot to your mother."

"Alright, but it won't be the same without you doing The Duke."

Disappointed, Kayla turned to leave. John continued to sand the deck. After a moment, he paused, watching his daughter slump out of the garage. He stood and walked bowlegged to the front of the boat, posing like a badass, holding his sanding pads at his sides like imaginary pistols.

"Young fella," John said in his terrible, twangy John Wayne voice, grabbing Kayla's attention. "If you're looking for trouble, I'll accommodate you. Otherwise, leave it alone."

Kayla smiled at their shared moment. Her spirit restored, she walked out of the garage to rejoin her family.

John reached down to his cell phone docked in the boom box and turned up the blues music. Bessie Smith's voice soared, echoing off the walls. She nearly covered the sound of his cell phone ringing. Startled, his hand passed the phone in the boom box and answered his *other phone* hidden within his tools. He carefully looked through the one exposed window before speaking.

"I'm alone," he said. "I said I'm alone. Puck? Say something, Puck."

The calm, deep voice of "Puck" finally replied in a strange, disjointed drawl as if he were severely illiterate. "We ain't outta use names."

"I told you, I'm alone. I checked."

"Checks again, John Boy," said Puck. "We don' want no surprise like in last time. That's a biggun family you gots. Either ways, we ain't outta use no names."

John looked through the window again, satisfied that John Wayne preoccupied his family. "I'm good. Now talk."

"If you still wants it, I just now gots it. Right here wit' me."

Uneasy, John tried to squash his nerves. It was imperative that Puck not sense any hesitation from him. "Yes. You know I still want it."

"You fer sure? This is your official last chance fer a U-turn."

"Yes, I'm goddamn sure! They just started a movie. Now talk!"

"You familiars with Oberti's?" Puck asked.

"Oberti's?" John said, trying to recall the place. "They bulldozed Oberti's last year."

"The billboard still stands. Off Highway 15. Near be Wild Wash Road."

John quickly checked a large map pinned to the wall next to the houseboat. "Yeah, I know where it is. Passed it a million times. There's nothing out there."

"Yep. You meets me there."

"Now?" John said, incredulous. "Jesus, that's an hour's drive!"

"What movie?" Puck asked in his calm, deep drawl.

"What?"

"The movie your kin be watchin'."

"Um... John Wayne... *True Grit*. They just started..."

"Good," Puck said, no trace of emotion in his voice. "Nice long western. You leaves now, stomp the gas, you can makes it."

"You can't be serious." John desperately tried to hide his sudden panic.

"I be there in an hour. An hour plus fifteen or so, I be gone, and ever'thing gets undone."

"Fuck fuck fuck!" John checked the time again. "Alright! One hour. Wild Wash Road."

"You brings my money," Puck said. "Prolly some more."

Before John could think of a reply, Puck hung up, returning John to his radio blaring old blues. He lowered the blinds on the one exposed window, cranked up Bessie Smith to a deafening volume, and locked the door Kayla used to return to the house.

Exiting through the massive garage door, John stepped out onto his driveway and made his way down to the street. His upscale home behind him, he readied the keys to an awaiting Ford Explorer a few houses down. With one last look around to ensure no one was watching, he sat behind the wheel of his SUV and started the engine.

Driving down Highway 15 at night always felt eerie to John, with only surrounding hills and fields as far as he could see. He was especially unnerved that night. Along the stretch, Highway 15 had no street lights, no traffic, no civilization. John heard no sounds of any kind save his Explorer's engine. Only rocky dirt and the occasional boulder could be seen for miles, as if he was driving to the end of the world. With the radio silent, he peered ahead through thick fog until his destination finally came into view.

A crumbling, old billboard appeared on a hill above him, to the left. It boasted of a happy family rest stop that no longer existed. The tall, red words "Oberti's Restaurant" beckoned him from a hilltop, a giant, rusty coffee cup still rotating along the top. No one had bothered to turn off the billboard's motor when the Oberti family business folded.

The exit for Wild Wash Road was just ahead. John turned off the highway and steeled himself for anything.

Wild Wash was a busted-up, decrepit road that climbed a slope. He left the road and continued to the hilltop, driving across a gravelly field to the rear of the billboard where a classic black Buick Riviera sat in Oberti's shadow, a few feet shy of the moonlight. A man in a quarter-length leather coat, jeans, and boots leaned against the old Buick, his cigarette burning along with his patience.

John parked a short distance away, shut off his engine, and stepped out of his Explorer, lugging a heavy duffle bag with both hands. He looked up at the old motorized coffee cup, creaking and screeching like a dozen knives dragged across a chalkboard, forever spinning for hungry families that would never come. The haunting sound pierced the night as he approached the black Buick.

"This better be good, Puck," John said, breaking their silence.

Patrick "Puck" Bains stood tall and lean, enshrouded in cigarette smoke. His dark brown hair dangled atop his shoulders and over most of his weathered face. He scrutinized John as he approached.

"You picked a helluva meeting spot," John said. "You sure this is secure?"

"You tells me."

"Puck... Mr. Bains... why don't we..."

Puck held his hand up "stop" and gestured for John to follow him to the rear of the billboard, away from his Buick. "I told ya, we ain't outta use names."

"Sorry. Look, Puck... I mean... I need to get back. I don't have time for..."

Without warning, Puck frisked John from top to bottom. He unbuttoned his shirt, reached in, and patted his chest. "Now we secure. You still fer sure you wants this?"

"Why the fuck are you still asking me that now?" John said. "Wasn't my 'last official U-turn' an hour ago? I got about 45 minutes before..."

Puck reached into his leather coat for a ski mask. He put it on, concealing his face.

"Wait, what's that for?" John asked.

"If'n case you gets cold feets."

"No way. No cold feet here. Now get on with it."

Without another word, Puck walked John to the trunk of his Buick. He unlocked it, pulled it up and open, and gestured for him to come look. John carefully stepped forward and peered inside.

Across the massive trunk laid a middle-aged man, tied up and gagged, balding with a tussled comb-over, his tortoise shell horn-rimmed glasses awkwardly angled across his sweating face. His eyes showed terror as he squinted up at the two men looming over him, the moon casting them as frightening silhouettes. They looked like the shadows of demons.

Equally frightened, the sight of the bound man paralyzed John. He felt nervous, scared, but kept his poker face, the illusion that he held all the cards. His initial shock faded quickly. Soon, he couldn't help but grin at his helpless victim.

"Hello, James," John said. "So nice of you to come. What a lovely, clear night."

From within the trunk, James Moorhouse looked up from his disadvantage. Recognizing his business partner, his eyes instantly changed from fear to fury. John relished it.

"You're uncharacteristically quiet," John said. "This might be the first time I haven't heard insipid bluster pour out of your pathetic face." John paced at the edge of the trunk, his voice and ego rising together in a crescendo. "All those years of bending me over and fucking the respect – the cash, the reputation – out of the business that I built! From nothing! And here you are, with nothing to say."

Silenced by duct tape wrapped around his head and across his mouth, James could only stare up at John in silent rage as he continued to torment him.

"I made you a wealthy man," John said. "Me! You owe everything to me! My ideas! My vision! But the rest of the world thinks that I'm the poor sap who owes you! Even my children think you're a rock star! That bullshit stops tonight!"

John's rage flamed as he eyed his partner's Patek Philippe watch, Brooks Brothers shoes, and Desmond Merrion pinstripe suit. Standing out in the lavish outfit, a golden four-leaf clover dangled from a delicate chain necklace. John reached into the trunk and ripped it off James's neck, wrapping it around his hand to taunt him. He grunted in disgust as he also took the platinum watch and alligator leather dress shoes.

"Look at all this!" John said, holding the luxury items in front of James's face. "$1,000 pair of shoes. $30,000 watch. $10,000 suit! All of this gaudy shit was bought with money from my hard work. Mine! It all belongs to me!"

John wanted to see pure fear in his partner's eyes. He hid his dissatisfaction at seeing mirrored rage instead. "Don't go anywhere, James," John said. "We're still trying to decide what to do with your sorry ass." John forced a laugh and slammed the trunk shut. He tossed the shoes to the ground and looked at the jewelry in his hands. Still high on adrenaline from the long-awaited moment, he turned to Puck. "So, now what?"

Puck took John back to the billboard, out of James's earshot. The creaking of the rotating coffee cup became deafening.

"Well, that be on you," Puck calmly replied.

"On me? Look, Mr. Bains... Puck... I'm new to this. You're the one..."

"I done my job, John Boy. From in this point, you picks what happens."

"What happens? What can happen? He's seen us!"

"He seen you," Puck said, his ski mask still covering his face. "Kinda limits your options, now don' it?"

"You're goddamn right it does!"

"See, John Boy, you didn't really thinks this through. All thems nights dreamin' 'bout gettin' revenge on your partner, thems fantasies never played out passin' this point, did they? You gloats, you stands over him, sees him shit his pants. You plucks the silver and gold toys from his body, sees him pissed off helpless. But what comes next?"

John's mind raced as he looked back to the shut trunk of the Buick. "What do you suggest? I mean, what normally happens now?"

"Normally?" Puck said as he tossed his spent cigarette to the ground, crushing it with his boot. "Ain't no 'normal' heres."

"What are my options?"

"A... You kills him. B... You lets him go, and deal wit' the cons'quence. C... I kills him, buries him in a hole somewheres 'tween here an' Vegas. Simple. 'Course, 'C' gonna costs extra."

"After what I've already paid you? Don't you dare blackmail me!"

"You only paids me half," Puck said, commanding control of the moment. "And it ain't blackmail, John Boy. It's options. Bid'ness. You gotta makes a choice."

John suddenly found himself frozen in indecision, overwhelmed and unsure about his next move. Puck saw the lost expression on his face and headed back to his car.

"Wait, where are you going?" John asked.

"Gonna takes Mr. Moorhouse home. You ain't got no guts, John Boy."

"How dare you speak that way to me."

"For reals, tho'. I'm gonna takes him wherever he wants to goes, like a taxi in the night."

John quickly tossed the duffle bag to the ground in front of Puck, halting him. "Alright!" John said. "Your other half and your 'some more' is in there. Now shut up and help me think of what to do!" John's eyes were wide and wild with desperation. He hoped Puck would think of something before cold feet came running.

Puck looked through the duffle bag full of cash. Satisfied, he returned to his car. As he popped open the trunk he saw John walking back to his Explorer.

"Theres coupla things I can do," Puck said. "But you stays."

"Like hell I am."

"You stays an' watch. You don' gets to walks away an' hears of it later. Gotta sees it for reals."

"Dammit, Puck, that was never the arrangement! I pay you, Puck, or Mr. Bains, or whatever the hell you call yourself! That means I'm in charge!"

Puck handed him back his duffle bag. John immediately tossed it onto the roof of the Buick, as if it sickened him to hold it a moment longer. He took Puck aside and lowered his voice. "You're out of your tiny mind, you know that, Bains? Okay, I'll stay. What are you gonna do?"

"I gonna do this." Puck pulled off his ski mask and reached into his coat again, this time pulling out a pistol. He pointed it at James in the open trunk.

"Hold on, Puck," John said. "Just hold on for..."

BLAM! BLAM!

With two shots point blank to the head, and a spatter of blood erupting at Puck and John, James Moorhouse laid dead in the trunk of the black Buick Riviera.

John couldn't believe what had happened. He suddenly became nauseous, falling to his knees, dry heaving with his face inches from the dirt. He could never have been sure how this would all end, but in the myriad of scenarios that had long spun in his mind, he inexplicably didn't once foresee this fatal outcome.

"What the fuck?" John yelled. "I just wanted to scare the bastard!"

"Believe you me, he was scared."

John muffled a scream, ready to rip out his hair. "There must be a million ways to terrorize a guy shitless! A million ways to press him under your thumb and take control so he'd never dare try to take what was rightfully mine ever again. But all of that is moot now, because you fucked us! Because you killed him!"

"Because you kept callin' me 'Puck.'"

The killer slammed the trunk shut, snatched the duffle bag from the roof of the car, and sat inside behind the wheel. With John still kneeling on the ground in silence and shock, Puck started the engine. He rolled down the window and checked the time on the dashboard.

"John Wayne jus' killed Ned Pepper," Puck said.

Trembling, confused, the bloody image of his former business partner still fresh in his mind, John looked up at Puck in his car. "What was that?" he said in a murmur. "John Wayne?"

"If you heads back now, you be with your family when he says goodbye to Mattie Ross, jumps that fence on his Chestnut horse, an' rides off in the snow."

In a whirlwind of panic, John wobbled to his feet. He quickly unwrapped his partner's gold four-leaf clover necklace from his hand as if it were a venomous snake and shoved it in his coat pocket along with the watch. Lost for words, he looked at the cold killer for any kind of solace, as if he could rewind time.

"Young fella," Puck said in his calm drawl, "if you're lookin' for trouble, I'll accommodate you. Otherwise, leave it alone." The familiar dialogue left John speechless and afraid.

Puck shifted into gear and drove away, the moon reflecting off the shiny black roof of his Riviera. Within moments, the distant sound of the old Buick faded to silence.

John Callender stood alone in the dark.

The old coffee cup rotated and creaked above him.

After racing back down Highway 15, John returned his Ford Explorer to its same spot on his street, a few houses away from his sprawling home. He used a remote control to open the garage door a few feet, just enough to duck under it and return to his houseboat.

The booming, echoing voice of Bessie Smith continued as John shut the garage door behind him. He whipped off his coat and tossed it up onto the deck of the houseboat. He washed the blood off his hands and face in the utility sink, made a beeline for the door to the house, unlocked it, and pulled up the blinds on the one window that looked into his house.

Exhaling in relief, he watched his family take in the last scene of John Wayne's Rooster Cogburn mounting a Chestnut horse, tipping his hat to a young Mattie Ross, and riding off toward the horizon, bounding over hills of fresh snowfall. Everything unfolded just as Puck described.

His family's favorite movie, *True Grit*, had just ended.

Bessie Smith crooned the chorus of *Gimme a Pig Foot and a Bottle of Beer,* the last song of her three-hour "Greatest Hits" album.

John's timing was perfect.

It felt meant to be.

Satisfied that his wife and children were completely unaware of his absence, he climbed onto his Seigneur de la Mar to return to his task of sanding its cherry oak deck. His heart stopped when he saw young Kayla kneeling beside his coat, sanding pads in hand.

"Kayla," John said. "How'd you get in?"

"I climbed through the window," Kayla said. "You pulled the blinds but didn't lock it."

"I see. How long have you been in here?"

"I don't know where you went, but I when I saw you were gone I figured I'd finish the deck for you."

Judging from the amount of work done, John surmised his daughter had been in the houseboat for nearly an hour, the entire time he'd been away. "I told you I had this. I told you to watch the movie with your mother."

"I know, and I told her you needed help," Kayla said. "She said it was cool." The girl handed her father his coat, dusting sawdust off it as she held it out. "What about Uncle James?"

"What about him?" John asked, trying to hide his nerves.

"He was supposed to come over and watch the movie. He never showed. I called him, but he didn't answer. I figured you guys must have met. You always have business stuff to talk about."

John paused for a moment and felt his nerves subside as a cover story came into focus. "You're right. I got a call from Uncle James. More business stuff to go over, always more business stuff. But I told him I gave myself the night off and was dedicating it to the boat and to you guys. He decided to work at the office without me. I went out for a beer, something better than the Coronas in the fridge. Uncle James always says I have a poor man's taste in things, so I ventured out to have a couple of pints of the good stuff at Wilbur's Tavern down the road. I had some kind of barrel-aged porter thing. The bartender said it was their best, so I treated myself. I gotta say, it was hard lifting a beer glass with my arms sore from sanding all day! But hey, even your old man needs a break now and then, right?"

"So, you didn't meet with him?"

"I just told you I didn't," John said. "Why? Did he call?"

Kayla wasn't sure what to think. She reached into her shirt pocket and revealed a necklace adorned with a small, golden four-leaf clover. "This fell out of your coat just now," he said. "When you threw it in the boat." Unsure, the girl held the necklace out to her father.

John took the necklace, startled to see blood on her daughter's fingertips.

It was blood from the golden clover.

"We gotta give it back to him tomorrow," Kayla said. "Uncle James says he always has my Good Luck Lure with him wherever he goes."

John couldn't move or speak. He thought to point out that lots of people had necklaces like this, that four-leaf clovers were common, and that maybe this belonged to him. The flimsy lie faded when he turned the cross over in his hand and saw two words inscribed across it...

Uncle James.

"Sure thing," John said. Cornered, out of ideas, out of stories, his shaking hand pocketed the bloody necklace. "Tomorrow."

The Nowhere Gate

The golden glow of the setting sun reflected off the old metal sign, turning its flaking white paint nearly red. The two stenciled words "KEEP OUT" shouted in stark black letters.

The sign stood obscured by weeds, but it didn't matter, for Dominique and Jess were at the age where such warnings wouldn't get in the way of a good time. Their faded blue Jeep sped past the sign as they rambled over winding, cracked pavement. Jess loved the feeling of driving that old 4x4 with its top down, but the novelty had grown tiresome with her friend. Dominique hated bouncing in the passenger seat over every rock and rut, her hair whipping upward in a whirlwind, her perfume long faded.

"Pretty sure this gonna turn out to be bullshit."

"It'll be worth it," Jess said, yelling over the roaring engine.

"This ride alone is bullshit."

"Do me a favor, Dom. Try to have some fun for once."

Dominique Powell's fans knew her as "Dom The Bomb" on the softball field, her underhand pitches able to break the sound barrier, but her sorority dubbed her "The Beast," fittingly describing both her physical prowess and her work ethic. With four other sisters recently graduated and gone, Dom had the distinction of being the one "good ol' fashioned black girl" in Delta Sigma Theta. Everyone regarded the stocky athlete as a fearless Amazon, a no-nonsense girl you wanted on your side in a conflict, a friend who often threw caution aside to stand up for herself and others.

In contrast, Jessica Holland's "fans" knew her as "Jess The Mess," a quirky girl who made funny one-woman sketches online, each garnering a few dozen views a week. Perhaps in defiance of her strict upbringing or her childhood as a wallflower, she spent nearly all her energy on becoming a social media butterfly. She saw her sketches as a stepping stone toward her goal of becoming a filmmaker, but despite her best efforts at self-promotion, none of her fellow sisters clicked Like or Subscribe. They regarded her simply as the sorority's Acolyte. Jess took pride in being Dominique's best friend since childhood and in being the book-smart "homegrown skinny white girl" of the sorority, following every trend and joining any club, party, or movement that would have her.

If only they had stuck to their perceived stereotypes that morning.

The crumbling single-lane road cut through an area of the foothills known as "The Sawmill," so named for reasons long forgotten since there was no sawmill in sight. Perhaps one stood long ago only to be razed so thoroughly that no evidence betrayed its former life. There was nothing at all aside from endless fields of tall grass and weeds, the occasional acacia tree, and the cracked, narrow, road that zig-zagged through it all. An inspiring sunset an hour's drive from civilization was The Sawmill's chief attraction, a sight that supposedly made one drop their liquor in awe. The comfort of enjoying that liquor with friends in complete seclusion was another draw, at least for those under the legal age.

Dominique and Jess were a couple of years shy of the law, but that seemed to be the point of prime partying. A touch of forbidden fruit usually sweetens the pot.

That day felt different.

"Forget bullshit, this is weird," Dominique said, clinging to the roll bar of the off-road convertible. "It's like one of those places you're used to seeing in movies but find creepy in real life."

"Hills and trees are creepy?"

"It's way too isolated, way too quiet."

"Great place to shoot a movie, actually," Jess said, making another right turn followed by a prompt left. The commanding road offered no choice.

"Every place is a movie shoot with you."

"Seriously, girl, no sound issues, plenty of room for trucks and equipment, and just look at this road."

"I would if I could," said Dominique.

Indeed, she could not. The grass and weeds stood so eerily tall, like an eternal cornfield – often higher than their raised Jeep – that only the bits of the twisting and turning road directly in front of them offered a view of their path. The pavement would briefly stretch until the next sharp turn, then onto the next. They had no clue which direction it took them until they were there, the wildly spinning compass on the dashboard providing no aid.

"And that's just it," Dominique said, grabbing the roll bar, standing up in the moving convertible to look around. "The road ahead is invisible, and we've been driving for almost an hour, top speed."

"Top speed in a Jeep ain't saying much." Jess laughed.

"Why didn't we take your car? It has a hell of a lot more horsepower than this old tank. Does Enrique even know we took it?"

"I would never submit my precious Mustang to a busted-up road like this!" Jess said. "And Enrique's busy with his Super Bowl party. He doesn't care if we have Old Blue. Hell, he has no right to care. I lent him half the money to buy it! I drive her all the time."

"Yeah, well 'she' drives like hell."

Upon spotting a twisted white oak atop a boulder, Jess slowed the vehicle to watch it block the setting sun, creating a striking glow through its dense foliage. It offered more material for a movie, or at least her blog. "Golden hour," she said. "I gotta take a picture."

"Of course you do."

Jess stopped the Jeep, stood atop her driver's seat, and took a photo of the lonely oak with her phone. She tried to post it online with the caption "Out in the sticks today, hope we make it back alive!" Sadly, there was no cell signal that far out into The Sawmill. "Dammit. So much for my live stream."

"Shit, that's really why we're here," Dominique said, angry at the realization. "This is another one of your damn location scouts or streams or whatever you call it. I thought the party would be bullshit, but there is no party, is there?"

"Well, there usually is. We just haven't found it yet. Gotta have faith, Dom!"

"Naw, this place is dead, faith or not. It's nowhere. The next turn could plunge us off a cliff for all we know."

"No way," Jess said with a snort.

"Or something else. Anything could sneak up on us out here. We should have stayed home at Enrique's Patriots party. You could have live-streamed that."

"My followers don't care about football," Jess said. "And might I remind you that the idea was to make our own fun for once, not piggyback on the boys' plans, or anyone else's." She plopped back into her seat, shifted into Drive, and continued down the broken road. "We don't need no man to have a good time, remember?"

"Sure, I remember," Dom said, "but this wasn't what I had in mind."

Before another word, the girls made one last turn and found themselves confronted by a towering, rusted ranch gate, only twenty feet in front of them. The sight of the towering structure somehow snuck up on them. In the wide expanse of fields, Jess stopped the Jeep for a few more photos. They pondered the structure in silence, at how the massive gate somehow eluded them until the moment they were staring at it.

"I thought you said The Sawmill road kept going to a dead end, next to some river," Dominique said.

"The Stanislaus River," Jess clarified. "And I never said that. I've heard other people talk about it. One of them mentioned that they never reached the end. No one has. We crossed the Stanislaus a while back, anyhow."

"Shit. Let's get out of here."

"So much for creating our own adventure," Jess said, muttering. "Damn, you're dead set on mingling with Enrique's frat brothers yet again. Or maybe Eddie's MMA wannabes? Where's that legendary Dominique Powell spirit of exploration?"

"It bounced out of the Jeep about five miles back."

Jess coasted the off-road vehicle toward the ominous gate. Its corroded steel pipes reached to the sky, holding up a carved wooden sign whose writing was lost to the elements. Perhaps it read in another language, it was so illegible. What made the gateway peculiar was the way it stood tall and completely alone, with no fencing left or right to keep out trespassers. One could simply walk around the rusted giant.

"It's getting dark," Dominique said. "Let's bolt. I got finals anyway."

"Hold on, Dom," Jess quickly said, not taking her eyes off the metal structure. "I've never heard about this gate. We might be the first ones to come out this far."

"Christ, it didn't erect itself," Dominique laughed. "Don't be a drama queen, Jess."

"I mean someone other than the owner. Aren't you curious to know who? Who would live way out here? No farmland, no power lines. Completely off the grid. It's more than an hour away from anything."

"Some people value their privacy," Dominique told her, disguising her hesitation with impatience. "We should respect that privacy, especially when it's this extreme."

Jess shut off the Jeep's engine and promptly hopped out, enjoying the feeling that, for once, she seemed genuinely more adventurous than her tough, local-legend friend.

Dominique removed her seat belt and stood up in the convertible. "Come on, let's go before it's dark. There's no street lamps out here."

"So?" Jess said, not really paying attention.

"So, it's creepy enough out here during daylight. The sun's going down. I don't want to drive this road five miles per hour in pitch black darkness. It'll take forever to get home."

Jess walked to the gate, looking it up and down, playfully touching the flakes of rust as if they were crystal. "You know what that old Jeep makes in gas mileage, Dom?"

"Probably shit."

"I wanna get my gas tank's worth. I didn't pay 70 bucks for a fill-up just to make a long distance U-turn."

Reluctantly, Dominique hopped out of the vehicle and joined her emboldened friend at the silent gate, leaving her passenger door swung open. They examined its weathered steel tubing, which sang to them in the chilling wind. Jess stepped onto the gate and started to climb.

"Just go around it," Dominique said. "You look ridiculous climbing over a big ass gate with no fences around it."

"It's no fun unless you feel like you're breaking a rule," Jess said, taunting. "I got that from you. But I guess that's the past, right?"

"A long time ago, sure." Dominique headed for the side of the gate.

"There are people who still climb things, long after their childhood," Jess said with a loud sigh, "and there are people who slowly walk around like the good, obedient ladies they're expected to be. I guess 'Dom The Bomb,' the feisty girl I grew up with, has surrendered to Miss Dominique Powell, the mature, proper, civilized woman. Nothing wrong with it, I guess, but it's like seeing Huck Finn grow up and get a job in a cubicle.

"There's my drama queen again."

"I'll always be your queen!" Jess said. "Seriously, it's just sad, that's all, seeing you tamed."

Dominique grimaced and relented, reaching her limit of taunting. Following her friend, she jumped onto the gate and scrambled up, swung her body over in a wide arc, and swiftly landed on the other side before Jess even reached to the top.

"Show off!" Jess laughed, her skinny arms and legs still struggling to climb. She reached the top, hoisted one leg over, and paused for a moment. She wanted to catch her breath, take in the view, and enjoy a moment of personal victory. It didn't matter that Dominique beat her at something for the thousandth time. It felt comforting, seeing her cut loose and become that fearless, reckless girl she grew up with, if only for a moment. "Good to know I haven't lost you yet."

While sitting atop the giant gate, Jess saw the look of concern on her friend below – even a trace of fear – as she stared through the gate's rusted bars. Jess inched her way down and landed awkwardly on the ground beside her. Before she could ask what the distressed face was all about, she caught the sight that disturbed her friend.

On the other side of the gate, Old Blue should have sat parked only twenty feet away.

It was gone.

The girls felt a stunned panic run through them with a chill. There was nothing but weeds and the setting sun as far as they could see, yet someone had stolen the Jeep with no noise, no trace.

"Jesus Christ, where'd the Jeep go?" Jess said with a tremble.

"They took it," Dom said.

"They?" Jess peered through the gate. "Impossible. We had our backs turned for thirty seconds. And what do you mean 'they'? Did you see them?"

"No, but do you really think one guy could have done this?" Dominique climbed halfway up the gate and yelled, "Who's out there?" unafraid of who might answer. "Where are you?"

Silence. The girls looked at the miles of nowhere again, the disturbingly tall grass and weeds able to hide anything.

"So, what happened?" Jess said, mumbling.

"The second we got out of the Jeep, two or three guys popped it in neutral and pushed it into the grass. They're hiding out there right now."

"And you're screaming at them?" Jess whispered, shivering from her friend's undeniable logic.

Dominique's hand raced into her back pocket for her phone. Before she could decide on who to call, she saw there was no signal out here. She looked behind her to the road continuing up into the hills. The grass wasn't so unreasonable on that side of the gate, just a foot tall. It seemed the safer of the two worlds.

"What are we gonna do?" Jess whispered again. "We're gonna get jumped in about ten seconds."

"We go up into the hills."

"Why? What's up there?"

"Something. Someone. This gate can't be here for nothing."

"It's older than God!" Jess said, expecting hands to grab her from behind. "I ain't going up there! That could be where the thieves live!" The fear in Jess's voice was pure, unfiltered, all bravado fallen away.

"Those hills are closer than anything out here," Dominique said, "and I'm betting someone lives up there with a working phone."

"You don't know that!"

"I'm going up. You can wait in the weeds if you want." She started up the road, walking backwards at first, keeping an eye open for anything.

"But Dom..."

"Night's coming. We gotta move."

Jess felt an icy wind slide across her, a sting that grew closer to pain the farther away her friend was. She resigned that Dominique had the right idea and followed as she always did.

As they continued up the road, the girls unfortunately failed to notice another disappearance – along with the absence of Old Blue was the absence of its tire tracks.

The pavement continued to crumble away as they hiked higher and deeper into the hills until there was nothing but loose dirt under their feet. The road became a trail, and the trail became lost in the thick woods that enveloped them past the first rise. At that point, the gate was well beyond sight, as was any part of The Sawmill's desolate fields. They now walked in a dense forest, the front yard of whoever erected the gate.

"How are we gonna get back?" Jess asked, exhausted. "There's no way we're finding the trail again. Every inch of these hills is covered with foot-high grass."

"We'll find it," Dom said. "I know where we are."

"Are you an Eagle Scout now?" Jess asked.

Dominique looked around for anything distinct. "That tree with the knot in it, looks like a Coke bottle. We'll look for that. The trail starts nearby."

"Fat chance we'll find it again. There're thousands of trees, same size, same color and shape. I can't see us spotting a single Coke bottle in all this."

"We'll find it," Dom affirmed. "I'll find it." Her tone betrayed frustration with not only their predicament, but with her friend's defeatist attitude and, frankly, her annoying lack of backbone, something that's plagued her since they were kids.

* * *

"So what are we looking for again?" Jess asked, spent from nearly an hour of trudging through the woods, the trail long gone.

"Anything. Just keep your eyes open. Those guys that swiped the Jeep might be up here."

"Hell, we might walk into their hideout," Jess said, muttering, as she spotted a small cabin ahead, sitting in the woods as if hiding from the rest of the world. "Dom, this is nuts. Let's turn back."

"Listen to you, girl. 'Hideout'. You watch too many movies. Think for a moment. The sun's below the hills. In a few minutes, these trees will drop us into darkness. We need to see if someone's home."

"This is nuts," Jess said again, shaking her head.

"This was the point of us hiking up here."

Jess stood silently as Dominique approached the cabin's door, planks of rotted wood held together with iron bolts. Upon closer view, she noticed it was ajar.

"Don't go in," Jess said, pleading in a whisper. She knew it would be her last chance to persuade Dominique to become a sensible coward like her, to return to the safe, tame girl she mocked earlier. "At least wait for me."

Together, the girls entered the old cabin. As decrepit as the exterior was, the interior had it beat with years of thick cobwebs covering overturned furniture and holes in the walls and roof. The inside seemed smaller than the outside, the cabin being wide and shallow.

The opening of the door cut through the darkness of the single room, letting in the faint sunset, brightening the cabin with a waning orange light. Jess remembered what Dominique said about the coming night and felt hurried to find help. "Is there a phone in here?" she asked, still whispering. "Maybe a signal?"

Dominique checked her phone – still no signal. She scanned the walls for anything. "There's nothing in here. This must be a storage shed or something, it's so small."

"What's that in the corner?" Jess bent down and picked up a small, tin, antique cookie box. Inside, she saw what looked like some oddly shaped fruit. It was soft and ripe, whatever it was, and it tempted her to eat it.

"What are these?" Jess asked. "Mutant apples?"

"Naw, probably just rotten." Dominique's voice hinted to hunger, and her companion shared the feeling. Quickly, Jess grabbed one fruit, examined it, took a bite.

"Get rid of that!" Dom said, slapping the odd shape from her friend's hand. But with the first swallow down, Jess felt assured that the food was harmless.

"Sour," Jess said. "Like old grapes. Still good. Hell, a ball of lard would be good now."

Joining in the careless abandon, Dominique bit into one of the irregular "apples." The girls ate slowly at first, as though the speed at which they dined would discourage any poisons present. After a minute, they sped their meal until the tin was empty like the rest of the one-room cabin.

During their uneasy snack, they failed to notice the last remnant of light fading behind the hills. It left the girls alone in the dark cabin, barely able to see each other. Standing in the open doorway helped, however, as the rising moon was full that evening, contrasting through the silhouettes of the giant trees.

"We should stay here tonight," Dominique said. "We can figure out this mess in the morning."

"You are nuts! I ain't staying here! What if the gang comes back?"

"A gang that lives in a shack on a box of rotten fruit?"

"Then someone else will come back," Jess said.

"That's what I'm hoping."

BOOM!

A chunk of the doorway's frame near Dominique's head suddenly blew apart with a piercing crunch that echoed across the trees. Wood shards flew into the air, and the girls immediately dropped to the ground.

BOOM!

Another piece of the cabin doorway shattered. This time it wasn't out of the blue, and they could hear things better.

Someone was shooting at them.

Judging from the holes in the wall, a shotgun did the work.

BOOM! BOOM!

of Gods and Devils and All In Between 135

"Jesus Christ!" Jess said with a shriek, drowned out by the constant gunfire. "It's them! Godammit, I told you!" She screamed obscenities into the dirt floor as she cowered, covering her head with her forearms, shrapnel scratching her neck.

"Let's go!" Dom shouted. "This way! Now!" She grabbed at her friend's hair and nearly dragged her crawling into a bush. Once obscured in the leaves, the firing ceased.

The sudden quiet was too much for Jess. "Leave us alone!" she cried, giving away their cover, triggering the rain of bullets to begin again.

BOOM! BOOM! BOOM!

The girls scampered through the woods, crouched low, constantly looking over their shoulders for their unknown stalkers. It was deathly dark, the moon barely able to pierce the dense brush. They felt for tree roots as guides across the terrain, making good speed and accuracy in their panic-fueled flight until Jess made the mistake of pausing for breath and falling behind.

BOOM!

Instantly, Jess felt the slug rip into her as she fell to the grass in a slow, dooming blur. Piercing pain streaked through her, though she didn't know exactly where she was hit.

BOOM!

Another dead-aim shot landed in the same place. Jess extended her leg into a sliver of moonlight and saw that the wound poured blood from her right thigh. The gruesome sight sent her into shock.

Dom saw the wound from her short distance away. She felt lucky that the powerful gun didn't completely sever her friend's leg. "Jess! Dammit, girl!" Dom whisper-yelled from what sounded very far away. To the ailing Jess, everything was growing more distant, muddled, faded.

Dom ran back to her, scooping her friend in her arms. The athletic girl lifted Jess and looked around to see if anyone was near.

With a turn of her head, Dom's eyes perfectly aligned with both barrels of a shotgun, protruding from the night, a few feet away away.

* * *

"Dom," Jess said, moaning as she woke, light stinging her eyes. "Dom, what's going on?" She gathered the strength to sit up, terrified to find herself back in the abandoned cabin. The dim room was the same as she remembered. At first she thought she was having a nightmare, but rather than seeing light from the sunset, she realized it was morning.

"Finally awake?" Dominique said, sitting cross-legged nearby.

"What happened? Why are we here? The last thing I remember..." Jess whipped the blanket off her lower body and saw her wound, now mended. It looked as though someone mummified her leg, her thigh wrapped amply with strips of green cloth. The dire scene came back to her. "They didn't kill us?"

"He," Dominique said. "He didn't kill us, for his own reasons. I don't know."

Still confused, Jess moved her leg, surprised at its condition. After the vicious wound she saw the night before, she felt sure she'd forever be crippled, if her leg could be saved at all. "What reasons?" she asked, becoming more confused as she fully awoke.

"I don't know, the guy doesn't talk. He..."

Dominique silenced herself as an old man entered carrying a pail and a shotgun. He was tall and thin with leathery skin, his body draped in a long black cloak. He looked like an ancient, bearded druid. To Jess, he may as well have been the Grim Reaper.

The shotgun sat well within reach of both girls, but they dared not touch it at the moment. Though it was clearly a weapon, Jess noticed it was odd in its design. It looked homemade, entirely metal, crudely constructed by an amateur welder.

"I thought you were another," the old man said in an unusual, elegant accent, enunciating each word like nails into wood. "I bring water. It's best to drink. It was a long walk."

"Dom," Jess said, mumbling, scared. "Tell me what's going on."

Her friend kept still and quiet as the old man set down the pail of water between them.

"Otim," the old man started, "I am Otim. I thought you were another. It is why I shot to you."

"You could've killed me," Jess said, realizing her morbid words as she spoke them.

"If I wanted your death, I would have it," Otim told the girls with no emotion. Jess couldn't disagree. She recalled the two shots hitting the same inch of skin on her running leg. The old man's marksmanship was without question. "I thought not about who you were until after I felled you," he continued, "and when I saw this other, holding you on the ground, I saw Ralina. I saw her for one moment."

The girls tried to hide their confusion, still afraid of the cloaked, dark figure of a man and his strange manner of speech.

"Ralina?" asked Dominique.

"I know now I saw wrong," Otim continued. "I should not have shot to you, no matter what the trees told me." Upon that, Otim exited the cabin, leaving the girls alone.

Jess turned to her friend in desperate confusion, hoping that whatever her friend was going to say would be good news. "Dom, tell me what the hell happened. Start at the moment I blacked out."

"I was deeper in the forest, far away from both you and... Otim. I thought you were with me. Then I heard you screaming in the distance. I swear, I thought you were right behind me."

"What about the old man?" Jess asked. "Why was he shooting at us?"

"He says he shot at us because he thought we were from the 'village board.' I don't know what that means. He didn't say another word until you woke up just now."

"Did you sleep?" Jess asked.

"A little. I tried not to, not with him around." Dominique dipped her hands into the pail of water for a drink. Jess followed, feeling a little better about it after seeing her friend's delicate trust in the old man. "There're no phones, no running water, no electricity. He's a hermit. Off the grid. Amish, if I didn't know different."

"How do you mean?" Jess asked. "The Amish don't shoot guns!"

"When I asked him about a phone, he didn't know what I was talking about. I described one to him, gestured with my hands, showed him mine. He just smiled and nodded. I might as well have been describing nuclear physics."

"He's nuts," Jess said. "He's goddamn senile. He took potshots at us for nothing and stopped for some nonsense reason. I look like Ralina? We gotta get outta here, girl. Right now. Let's find this village of his."

"I don't know. I mean, he wanted us dead, thinking we were from there."

"Because he's nuts!" Jess said, regretting her sudden raised voice. "What's more likely, that a hermit off the grid is crazy, or an entire village of people? They're his enemies, not ours. And maybe they got a phone."

"Or maybe they got the Jeep," Dom said.

"I thought I was the one who watched too many movies."

"This isn't fear, it's caution," Dom said, "and maybe a little fear."

"It would be stupid not to be afraid right now. Even you."

The girls quieted themselves when Otim returned carrying two large bowls of berries. He set them down and walked back to the doorway. "Leave when you wish it," he said, facing the trees. "Keep the anointed cloth on the leg."

"Thanks," Jess said with reservation, realizing that this insane man saved her life only after endangering it. Still, she felt grateful. She spoke carefully, trying to endear herself to the man. "This is some amazing stuff you put on me. Probably banned from the Olympics. I mean, I bet an hour from now I could run like a deer!"

"Then run home like deer," Otim said, leaving the cabin. "I patched you because I near killed you. This how far I help."

"We need more help," Dominique gathered the courage to say. "We're lost. Our Jeep... our wagon... was taken. Please, anything you can do. You know these hills."

"This how far I help," he said again as he headed out into the trees.

"Think of Ralina," Dom said, hoping to prey on his sentiment.

Otim didn't respond as he walked further into the woods. Jess felt relieved that the man refused to assist them. She still feared him, despite the cool and cautious tone Dominique had taken.

"Let's go now," Jess whispered, "before he switches personalities again." Dominique didn't feel as repelled as Jess did. Perhaps, she thought, if she were the one that was shot, she'd feel different.

Her leg healing but still a little stiff, Jess rose to her feet. Dominique helped her across the cabin, making her cross it twice again on her own. Satisfied with her nearly restored mobility, Jess joined Dominique at the door. They headed outside, found their bearings, and began their hike further up into the hills.

Otim watched them leave and thought about Ralina. The old man normally left folks to their own business, including those from beyond the trees, even though he knew their fates. He could normally rely on his stone heart to help him forget the two Others who broke into Ralina's old cabin and eaten the tribute he'd left for her, but they remained in his thoughts. The one with the leg wound reminded him so much of Ralina. Seeing her laying on that bed brought back memories of her final night.

Perhaps he should have killed the two Others or ensured that they returned to the nowhere place past the gate at the bottom of the hills. Either choice would have been a kindness compared to what awaited them in the village.

* * *

The village sat in a small canyon. A dozen thatched rooftops blended with the surrounding trees, a few seen against white boulders that sat near the entrance of the clearing. Some were small, round, windowless log cabins that rose from the ground like massive barrels, while others protruded from the canyon's cliff sides as if they'd been grown rather than built. Sculptures and carvings of bears, birds, wolves, and deer adorned the front of each cabin. A winding granite path bisected the village, connecting all the cabins, each entryway covered with either canvas or animal hide rather than wooden doors like Otim's.

Jess smiled like a tourist as she took in the charming details of the strange village. She didn't expect to see the odd structures organically built into the land, nor the many families donning black and gray clothing from another era. The men wore doublets, stockings, buckled shoes, and broad brimmed hats while the women wore smocks, waistcoats, coifs, and bonnets. In turn, the villagers didn't expect to see the girls in their strange modern attire, though they didn't share Jess's delight.

"It's like an historic theme park," Jess said under her breath, eyeing the villagers going about their day, a careful, almost fearful manner in their stolen glances.

"They haven't shot at us yet, so that's a good sign," Dominique said, feeling somewhat justified in leaving the foreboding old man to hike there. She evaluated each of the townsfolk for first contact, deciding that no one person seemed any more willing to talk with them than another. She randomly chose a small girl drawing on the path with a white rock. "Hey sweetie. Is there a phone we can use? Is there police around here? Someone in authority?" The girl looked confused. "Who's the big boss around here?"

The girl jumped to her bare feet and ran across the narrow central path to her mother who sat plucking chickens in front of the largest cabin. The two of them ducked inside through the cabin's canvas doorway. Jess heard the woman inside telling others about them. She couldn't make out her words, but her frightened tone didn't sound encouraging.

Dominique couldn't take her eyes off the wide water tank sitting in the middle of the village, its walls made of small birch trees tied together. It looked to be the focal point of the village. A towering well crane loomed over it, equipped with a long boom and several rows of tools hanging from ropes. Like Otim's gun, the tools had strange, hand-crafted designs to them, uninfluenced by the rest of the world.

"It's like these people stepped off The Mayflower 400 years ago," Dom said, "found a secluded, protected spot in this canyon, and never left it. I mean, they're looking at us like we're Martians."

"What happened to seeing too many movies?" Jess said, laughing at the notion of a forgotten village. The sight of children playing had put her at ease, a feeling her overly cautious friend didn't share. Jess walked into the large cabin the woman retreated to. Dominique remained at the doorway, alert and ready for the proverbial shoe to drop squarely on them.

"Hello, excuse me," Jess said as she entered the long, crowded room. It seemed to be some kind of public house. She saw tankards of beer being filled from small barrels, a boar roasting on a spit behind a granite bar, and the morbid sight of 50 deer heads mounted to the walls, their antlers decorated with leaves and flowers. Two dozen villagers stared blankly at her, eyeing the green wrap around her right thigh. "My friend and I need a phone. Please, can you help us?"

The villagers looked just as puzzled as Otim did earlier, but their curiosity felt different. No kind faces, no signs of sympathy. She didn't remind *them* of some girl named Ralina... or maybe she did.

"A phone, please, anything," Jess said. "A police officer? And there was a man who attacked us. He shot at us." She pointed to her wrapped wound.

Before she spoke another syllable, a tall, bearded man in a deep blue peacoat emerged from behind the bar, smelling of roast pork and burnt wood. He dragged a short wooden club across the granite counter, his eyes darting from the timid, skinny white girl in the denim shorts to the large black girl standing guard by the entrance. From the expressions and the air in the room, this man was clearly a pillar of the community, an authority figure.

The big boss.

"I'm Jess Holland. Over there is Dominique Powell."

"Azariah," the man in the peacoat said, his deep voice gripping the room. "I serve the trees as ward of the village."

Jess felt prepared to explain everything to Azariah, but hesitated when no one reacted when she mentioned that someone had shot at them. No one attempted to answer any pleas for a phone or help of any kind. Just the opposite, the villagers seem preoccupied with the more mundane things, such as the girls' appearance, their clothing, the way they entered the village unannounced and spoke before being spoken to.

In that moment, Jess realized that there was no actual entrance to the village. She and Dominique clawed their way through dense trees and heavy brush before finding the clearing. The idea of a village lost in time suddenly didn't seem so absurd. Requesting their help now felt like a risk rather than the obvious choice. But it was their only one.

"Why do you arrive?" Azariah asked. The villagers in the room awaited an answer.

"Our car was stolen down the road, by the gate. A blue Jeep. Maybe you saw it? We're stuck out here. We need a phone."

"Stolen?" he said, his voice bellowing, turning to the stunned villagers like a showman. "A crime?" Their gasps felt genuine, as if Jess's story supported some unfounded prejudice. "Someone stole from you? Beside a gate?"

"Yes, our car was stolen," Jess said word by word, as if she'd make more sense that way. She remembered Dominique's phrasing at Otim's cabin. "Our wagon was stolen by your gate, on the road that leads up here."

"The Gate to Nowhere is not ours," Azariah said, offended, his words landing firm in the minds of all around him. "That abomination was erected by Others from beyond the trees." He shut his eyes in prayer. The villagers bowed their heads.

"Yes, sure," Jess said. "Our Jeep was on the road next to it. Our car. You know, like a motor wagon?"

Azariah heard the strange words, read the hesitation and confusion in the room. No one understood nor did they care to try. The mere concept of a road seemed as alien to them as a car or a motor. That alone was enough to stoke their fears.

Thinking about Dominique's Mayflower comment, Jess recalled reading about communities like this in other countries, tribal people isolating themselves from civilization to the point that anything modern seemed bizarre, confusing, and therefore dangerous. These religious communities were comprised of sheltered zealots, their lives revolving solely around worship.

Anything different was a threat. She considered showing them a photo of the gate but didn't dare reveal the dark magic of her iPhone.

"Is there another village nearby?" Jess asked politely, pulling away, trying to hide her shaking hands. She quickly dismissed her irrational notions, telling herself that they weren't in the heart of Africa or the Amazon, reminding herself that she had indeed seen too many movies. Still, her fear felt palpable. "It's alright, we can get help somewhere else."

Azariah stood emotionless, staring at the strange girls in their unholy clothing, speaking of crime and things unfamiliar, things surely not crafted by God or His children.

Dominique pieced together in her head who the car thieves were, why Otim shot first and spoke later. Standing at the doorway, looking out at the village, her voice grabbed the attention of the room. "Jess, let's move on now. These people don't need us bothering them." Her words went unheard, the villagers sitting still in their silent judgement. As she turned from the doorway, the sudden absence of her friend frightened her. She could no longer mask her trepidation.

Before another word, hands clutched her from every angle, carrying her away.

She screamed as they lifted her off her feet.

Moonlight stretched across the stone floor in streaks of light and shadow, its beams interrupted by the metal bars on the door's window. The room obviously served as a jail cell, with walls made of stones embedded in a stucco-type substance. There were occasional small holes through the walls, showing the village and revealing the cell to be a free-standing structure, trees all around it.

Dominique knelt on the ground at the rear of the cell, trying desperately to break through a weak spot in the stucco with a small rock she broke in half, creating a sharp edge. Jess peeked through the door's barred window, listening to the villagers' evening meeting at the large water tank in the center of town.

"They come here for the same reason as the Others," one villager said. "They mean to violate our life. The trees have been crossed, there's no talk to have."

"Indeed," said another. "If they are allowed to leave they will return with more Others, and soon their numbers will be greater, out of balance. The trees have told us what to do."

"Yes, but how?" asked another. "How do we keep them here? Keep the balance?"

The villagers talked in groups, their concerned voices overlapping, making it hard for Jess to understand what they were saying.

"I decide how to cleanse the village," Azariah said, "as I have for 55 turns." His deep, commanding voice silenced everyone. "We must first cleanse these Others. The water will purify their bodies before they are set afire. We shan't have their diseases lingering in smoke over our sleeping homes. The trees have shown us this."

Jess gripped the window bars in terror as she continued to listen. She would listen only a minute more before joining Dominique in her desperate, seemingly futile task of breaking through the rear wall.

In that minute, however, another voice cut through the mob.

"The trees have told me different!" Otim said as he made his way through the gathered crowd. "The trees have told me that to end their lives is to soil us with injustice, an intolerance only to quell paranoia."

"An injustice?" Azariah said, scoffing at the impudent fool. "Such as that of your daughter?" The girls heard chatter in the crowd of the long dismissed incident, diminishing any faith in the old man.

"Ralina's death indeed remains an injustice," Otim said, "and though I abide the council's edict, I still see fear over wisdom."

"And that is why you are still banished," Azariah said.

"Ralina left the village out of curiosity, not malice!"

"On that, we agree," Azariah said for all to hear. "I believe she meant no harm when she ventured out of the canyon, even as she dared to defy God, to turn her back to His gifts and glory. But she returned and implored us to accept the world beyond, their witches and demons and machines of death. She brought forth the idea of clearing a path to allow those demons to visit upon us." Azariah paused, finding his next words acidic and vile. "She talked of cutting down the sacred trees to create that path! You must realize, Otim, she might have left us as your innocent, curious daughter, but she returned as an unholy Other. They bent and broke her to their will."

"That is not why I challenge!" Otim said. "Ralina's tale has been told and is done. My tale my own is done. But I say to you all now, let these new Others leave. They will die alone among the trees if that is what the trees wish."

"I assure you, that is what they wish," Azariah said, "for that is what they have told me. Knowing this, I see no reason to lengthen their misery any further. That, to me, would soil us with injustice."

"You dare speak of injustice?" Otim said, eyes aflame.

"And you dare speak to the village ward in defiance? The man appointed by God to protect us and speak to the trees? I now know why Ralina was so easily tempted and led astray. She turned because she is her father's daughter."

"I think I can get through!" Dominique said, almost too loud. Jess heard her, but returned to the barred window to hear their only defender's appeal.

"I refuse to let this transpire," Otim said, walking to the steps of the well. "We let the sun set on one child out of fear and cowardice, and once is more than this hallowed village deserves. Are we not a family? Do we not share our voices and thoughts?" Otim made his plea with logic and reason, and some villagers nodded in agreement, but Azariah heard only sacrilege and insubordination. To him, the plea for mercy was a challenge to the trees and to God, but most of all, it was a challenge to his authority,

Otim's fate was frighteningly clear to Jess. She scrambled back to the Dominique at the rear wall and jabbed the sharp rock into the thick, solid stucco. In their struggle, they heard the crowd shouting, their voices growing louder, shifting across the village clearing. Otim's screams echoed over the mob as they restrained and bound him to the well's long boom. Jess looked over her shoulder, back at Otim through the window.

Lowered over the water, the old man was submerged repeatedly, each time held under the surface far too long for any elderly person to endure. Still, he struggled to live, and Jess took it as an effort to buy more time for Dominique to pound her way out of that damn cell. The louder the crowd yelled, the harder she struck the wall, their angry voices covering their work.

Jess joined her in breaking off pieces of loose stucco. Though Dom was the strong one, Jess's fear fueled her to almost match efforts, her fingers bleeding from clawing through the cement-like wall.

"There, right there," Dominique said, keeping her voice low. "We've got it!"

"Did you hear any of what they were saying?"

"Believe me, I didn't miss a word."

As Otim took his final gasp for air at the village center, the girls made their way through the narrow hole and out into the forest. They knew the villagers would hunt them down the moment they discovered their escape. But the interior of the jail cell was largely cloaked in shadow, which might buy them still a little more time. All they could do was run as fast as they could back to the gate, catering to Jess's injured leg, hoping that the head start was enough.

"Start looking for the trail," Dominique said, panting as she ran.

"What are we gonna do when we get back to the gate?"

"I don't know, we'll see when we do it," Dom said. "The grass is ten feet tall there and goes on for miles. Maybe we can lose them in it." It was a flimsy plan, but they both knew there was no other way.

During the long night, they were relieved to hear no men or guns or dogs behind them as tried to advance through the woods. The relief turned to panic as they passed the same trees, the same clusters of berries, even approaching the village again. It seemed the small commune in the canyon was surrounded by cliffs and boulders from nearly all sides. If there was any way to flee the village, it likely entailed scaling the steep walls of rock, which Jess was in no condition for.

"We got in, there's gotta be a way out!" Jess said.

"Otim's cabin was just a few miles back that way," Dominique said, trying to piece things together. "We need to double back to there. The trail should be nearby."

"No, it was further."

In their conflicting mind maps of the area, they needed a sign. At the peak of their fear and desperation, they spotted one.

"The Coke bottle! This is it, right here!"

The twisted tree with the only distinguishing feature in sight pointed its one barren branch to the ground, revealing wild grass scattering across hardpan dirt with remnants of the busted pavement leading down to the trail.

The breakthrough came too late.

The moment the girls took their first step onto the broken trail, the paralyzing sound of dogs barking in the distance sent a chill through them. The villagers had discovered their empty cell and were in pursuit.

"We gotta run!" Dom said, her voice betraying her horror. "Run like a deer!"

"I can't! You know I can't!"

"You've got to!"

Dominique grabbed Jess's arm, tugging her along, an act she would normally never attempt on her delicate friend, but one that neither of them protested. Jess strained with each step, somehow making considerable speed through all the pain. Wincing from her burning leg, she found a new confidence on the downhill area as the path led away from the foothills, and released her grip on Dom. Her moment of hope fell apart when the cracked trail leveled as it approached the gate. It waited hundreds of yards away, much farther than she remembered, forcing the girls into the open across an exposed sprint to the endless, empty Sawmill. Their Jeep was gone, but there was an ocean of tall grass that could hide an armada, let alone two overwhelmed girls. The endless grass, once foreboding, stood as their only chance to lose the zealots racing closer.

"They're getting louder," Dominique said. "They're gaining!"

Halfway down that exposed stretch, the girls turned around to see the terrifying sight of a mob carrying long wooden poles and tools, being led by a team of dogs.

"We pass that gate, we keep running! Right into the grass!" Dom said.

The dogs yelped and barked, sounding more determined as they held the girls' scent. Jess realized the error of their plan, heaving as she struggled to continue. "The dogs, Dom! How the hell are we gonna hide from dogs?"

They kept pushing on, even as all hope faded away, even as they realized that there was never any hope to begin with.

Azariah marched forward at the head of the mob, near the pack of dogs. He wore a calm expression, a contrast to the dozen hostile, blood-lustful men that made up his hunting party. At the rear of the group, nailed to a log carried by several men, laid Otim's mutilated body. The torturous drowning in the tank served only as a prelude to whatever cruel ritual claimed his life.

The gate loomed on the horizon. Where it was eerie before, it was now a welcome sight, encouraging them to reach it for an impossible salvation. Dom and Jess couldn't tell how far away it was because of its immense size. The only thought in their minds was to keep running.

The villagers' wild screams grew louder as they narrowed the gap between them and their prey. The dogs' barking sharply rose and fell in volume, making Dominique run faster with each peak. She soon realized how much farther ahead she was than her crippled friend, just as she was the night before. This time, the lead was much greater. She never should have let go of her friend.

Jess felt the wound in her leg swell with heat. Blood trickled out from beneath the green wrap on her thigh, pumping out with each footfall. The healing cloth unraveled, and the wound pulsed blood onto the gravelly dirt. She expected to fall at any moment. She struggled as best she could, but at the end of an extensive surge of pain, she succumbed to her agony and collapsed to the ground.

Dominique also knew her friend's destiny to fall and heard it happen with an almost timed feeling. It was no less horrific to hear. She whipped around, prepared to run back to her, but as the thought formed in her mind the dogs had reached their target. Jess's cries for mercy were muffled by the vicious dogs tearing her apart like a rag doll.

Dominique screamed in terror. She froze as her mind snapped. Turning away from her friend's grisly death, she looked ahead to the waiting gate, unsure of what to do. The dogs decided for her as half of them broke away from the fallen Other and hurtled toward their new target. Dominique continued to run, making no effort to meter her speed in wait of her friend as before.

Getting closer to the gate, her heart ready to burst, Dominique saw barbed fencing stretching from both sides of it like an eternal periphery, an endless, formidable fence that impossibly wasn't there the day before. It only added to the barrage of fear and confusion and helplessness overtaking her.

The young woman lunged at the rusty metal gate, making it shake briefly, hanging on to it in complete exhaustion. The villagers closed in, their frenzied voices loud as if they stood next to her, screaming in what sounded like another language, a jumbled fog of hate and the enveloping roar of the dogs.

"Kill the Other!"

"Kill the witch!"

"Don't let her cross over!"

As Dominique wobbled on the top of the gate, the demon dogs leapt forward, latching onto her pants. They viciously destroyed denim like wet paper, losing their grip, and falling off her along with the shreds of fabric and ripped flesh. Her ears were filled with the oncoming chaos of the mob, and she was tempted to collapse to the dirt, surrendering to her unshakable fate.

Lynn Harrod

Ready to faint in the beating sun, she swung her bloody legs over the top of the gate and fell to the other side, landing on her stomach, hard to the ground.

Silence.

Dominique had given up. Her energy completely spent, she waited for something to reach her. A dog, a blade, the clutches of the men, but there was nothing.

The villagers were gone.

The dogs were gone.

Jess's riven body had disappeared.

Lying flat, face-down in the dirt, Dominique rose and looked about her, lost in a search for answers. She felt heat coming from her left. Her eyes quickly caught something that one would normally consider salvation, though she felt no comfort in its presence, only torment and despair.

Twenty feet from where she laid sprawled across the bloody ground sat Old Blue. The warmth of its dormant engine was still strong, its passenger door swung open as she had left it.

The Queen's Angel

Monday morning on the streets of St. Nelia during the summer months is not for the faint of heart. By nine o'clock, temperatures often hit the nineties. By noon, folks are trudging through triple-digit heat with thick, smog-infused humidity.

The St. Nelia District of the city, named for the small Gothic Revival church at its center, had seen far better decades. A decayed urban neighborhood on the edge of the industrial zone, it comprised 28 blocks of mixed-use retail, low-income housing, freeway on-ramps, railroads, electrical towers, liquor stores, and hole-in-the-wall cafes of every ethnicity, all covered with five barrios worth of graffiti.

On the southern outskirts of the district, the sun beat down on the Royal Queen Motel, a relic from the 1950s. The only remnants of the motel's glory days were its long-shuttered pizza parlor boasting of a "fully air-conditioned dining room" and its once-brilliant neon sign of a queen as tall as a telephone pole holding up a giant pale yellow star. Under sun-bleached acrylic glass, framed by rusted steel, her majesty's girl-next-door smile could still be seen after 66 years, the only detail of beauty left on the property. Gangs, homeless denizens, streetwalkers, and drug dealers stood in place of the traveling families that used to stop there on their way to the coast. Castle Avenue, the byway that once fed the motel a steady stream of tourists, was now derelict and lined with barbed wire.

Maria and Eduardo Ramirez, an elderly Mexican couple dressed in their Sunday best, walked across the motel's lot to the manager's office. The only car present was a lowrider, a faded, banged-up silver 1960 Chevrolet Impala that used to be a sweet show car but had long since been neglected by its owner. Car clubs and auto shows are no longer on the calendar when surviving day by day.

Maria rested on the front bumper of the Impala while her husband approached the office's walk-up window. Eduardo spotted the surly manager and tapped on the glass.

Carlos Cruz sat inside, a Latino covered with intricate tribal and crude prison tattoos, wearing a clean, white tank top, overpriced studio-quality headphones, and a permanent scowl. He zoned out to classic British heavy metal – Judas Priest, his guilty pleasure – while reading a *Cruising* car magazine, never looking up from its pages.

Eduardo adjusted his fedora only to remove it respectfully as he pushed forth the words he long dreaded. "I am Eduardo Ramirez," he said in Spanish. "This is my wife, Maria. Good morning, sir."

Carlos eyed the old woman sitting on his lowrider. It annoyed him to see someone rest on his ride like a common bench, but he let it go. He returned to his magazine.

"Is he here today?" Eduardo asked. "I was told he'd be here."

"Who" Carlos asked in Spanish, not taking his eyes off his magazine.

"The Angel."

"Who?" Carlos said, laughing, feigning ignorance.

"Please, sir, where is he?" Desperate, Eduardo slid a fifty-dollar bill across the window counter. Carlos promptly swiped the money and stepped outside.

Intimidating, lean, and muscular, the towering stone-faced young man dressed like a gangster in his tight tank top and baggy pants. He gestured for the old couple to follow him to a nearby room. Eduardo guided his confused wife.

"Don't negotiate," Carlos said without looking at the elders. "Don't mention money at all. It offends him."

Upon reaching Room 23, Carlos knocked on the door as he opened it. He remained at the doorway like a guard as the elderly couple entered. Eduardo stepped onto the flattened, stained shag carpet and looked around the room, a simple suite in wildly outdated decor that exuded style in the 1970s. He gestured for Maria to sit in a chair as he turned to face the mysterious man he'd been so anxious to meet.

Abel Grant, a middle-aged Black man in pressed jeans, loafers, and button-up shirt, entered from another room. He smoked a cigarette – as he constantly did – and spoke with an all-business tone of control. He offered Eduardo a handshake.

"My name is Abel Grant."

Eduardo shook Abel's hand and struggled to speak English. "Mr. Grant... do you remember... me? From St. Nelia church? Eduardo Ramirez. Please... you remember..."

"I remember you, Mr. Ramirez."

"Good," Eduardo smiled. "My wife Maria... she..."

Abel held up his hand, silencing the old man. "Did you pay Carlos?"

Both the mention of money and the use of English confused Eduardo. Abel realized his guest's lacking fluency and repeated himself.

"Did you pay this man?" Abel said, switching to rough Spanish.

"Yes," Eduardo said in Spanish, relieved that the "angel" spoke his language.

"How much?"

"Fifty dollars. I'm sorry, it is all I have. But I can get more."

Abel snuffed his cigarette in an ashtray on the bedside table and approached Carlos at the door. The giant gangster promptly handed over the cash. Abel leaned in close and stared down his imposing comrade. "If you take money from anyone ever again," Abel said in plain English, "we're done, and I will give back what I took from you nine years ago."

To Eduardo's surprise, the monstrous gangster couldn't look the angel in the eye. He bowed his head, staring down at the carpet in shame, as Abel returned the cash to the old man. He gestured for Maria to sit on the bed. Confused, money in hand, Eduardo did as he was told.

"Tell me," Abel said in Spanish.

"Forty years ago, we came to America together," Eduardo began. "Forty years of marriage, six children, many grandchildren... and now my love doesn't know my face." He held back tears. "Now she's lost to me! I don't know what to do! Our children have all moved away. All we have now is each other, just like in the beginning."

"How long?"

"A year," the old man said. "A very hard year. Doctor says she will only get worse."

"You understand she may be beyond my help?"

Eduardo nodded, tried not to cry. Maria was oblivious, dazed, as Abel gripped her hand, lifting her face so they were eye-to-eye.

"So pretty in your Sunday dress," Abel said to her. Maria looked at him. Unsure. Afraid. "Don't be scared, Maria. I'm going to do my best to take it all away." Though lost in a storm of emotion, Maria simply nodded "yes."

Abel held her hand a few different ways until he finally got it... *the feeling.* He shut his eyes and clutched Maria's hand. As the sensation grew stronger, Abel fell to one knee.

Eduardo moved to help, but Carlos stopped him.

Abel breathed heavily, as if a weight had been placed on him. Maria slowly turned and looked about the room. She locked eyes with her husband. Eduardo could see his beloved wife returning.

Abel finally released her hand, remaining on one knee. Maria approached Eduardo. Husband and wife embraced for the first time in months. Abel rose to his feet, exhausted. "How do you feel, Maria?"

"I feel... light," Maria said in Spanish.

"What's your name, my love?" Eduardo asked. "Do you know who I am? Do you know..." Abel gestured for Eduardo to calm himself, to give her a moment.

"I do know," Maria muttered. "I'm so sorry, Eduardo."

"It's not your fault." Eduardo abandoned holding back as tears streamed down his face.

Carlos looked down, failing to hide his own emotions.

"It's a miracle!" Eduardo exclaimed. "A miracle! God is good! I thank God!" He turned to his savior, beaming with a smile he hadn't felt in ages. His face had long felt rusted into an expression of sorrow but now was now freed from years of struggle and grief. "I prayed day and night, and God brought me to you! His angel!"

Abel stood unmoved. He reached for a new cigarette and spoke his rough Spanish slowly. Pointedly. "The city bus brought you to me. Your feet brought you to me. What God did was make her sick to begin with. You can thank Him for that."

"Yes," the old man recalled. "I was told you are angry with God. Reverend Dean says you don't need to believe to be in His eyes. I know He was here today, I know you are His angel, and I thank you."

Eduardo took out the fifty-dollar bill from his coat pocket again and tried to place it in Abel's hand, but he refused. "Reverend told me you need payment," Eduardo said, confused.

"Do you make anything for a living?" Abel asked.

Eduardo shook his head "no."

"Do you grow anything? Do you cook?"

"Maria bakes!" Eduardo said. "My love is the best! Anything you want! Cakes! Pies!"

"Bake me a pie."

Eduardo quickly agreed, a strange laugh escaping his lips. "She will bake you many pies! Cakes! Sweet breads! Anything you want!" Maria smiled proudly.

"Just one pie."

The simple request took Eduardo aback, but he hugged his angel in gratitude. Abel gestured for the door. As the couple walked out, Abel offered an ominous warning.

"Remember, Mr. Ramirez," Abel said. "Tell no one what happened here, not even your children. What I took from your wife... I do not want to give back."

Eduardo respectfully, fearfully, agreed. The couple walked out into the sun. Carlos followed but paused at the door.

"Sorry, Boss," Carlos said in English. "About the money."

"I'd think after nine years you'd know better."

"We coulda used that fifty. That's what I know. I was weak, but we gotta eat, Boss."

Standing in his barren, decrepit room, Abel couldn't argue. "You'll get first piece of that pie, my friend."

Carlos nodded and left with the old couple, shutting the door behind him.

* * *

The door to Room 23 opened again. As before, Carlos remained at the doorway as new visitors entered.

Angela Vega, a middle-aged Filipino woman, walked in with her son, Roberto, an angry young man just two months shy of his seventeenth birthday. She wore a sundress while her son proudly wore gang colors in baggy jeans and a tight T-shirt.

"You want me to speak to this fool?" Roberto asked his mother in Tagalog, a common dialect of Filipino.

"Be nice!" Angela said, barking at him in Tagalog. "This is a man of God!"

Roberto scoffed at the notion. Abel snuffed his cigarette and approached the teen, speaking to him in English. As before, he offered his hand as he introduced himself.

"My name is Abel Grant."

Roberto looked at Abel's extended hand for a moment before taking it. He didn't yet trust this "angel," nor did he understand what the hell he was doing there. "Roberto, Angela," the young man said, introducing himself and his mother. He grinned as he turned to the large man at the door. "And you're Carlos, right? Respect." Carlos nodded in recognition. Roberto turned his attention back to Abel. "My moms don't speak no English, but she gets it a little bit."

"And I get Filipino a little bit," Abel said, "so we're halfway to an understanding. Now, tell me."

Roberto found it hard to explain, as if it were all nonsense. "My moms says she's been having... seizures? She says you can help, that you're some kind of shaman, something like that?"

"Something like that."

"So, do whatever you do, I guess. She wants the seizures gone. It's news to me, but she says they're pretty bad."

Abel studied his guests. He saw the worry on Angela's face, how she kept looking at her son, and realized the truth. "She's not here for any seizures," Abel said.

Confused, Roberto stared at his mother until she finally broke her silence. She spoke hurriedly in Tagalog, as if the timing was critical. "His brother! Only eighteen when he joined the gang! Their father's gang!"

"What the fuck is this?" Robert said, stammering.

"Quiet!" Abel said.

"The police shot him! And he almost died!" Angela said, continuing. "Instead, he's in prison. Now my baby boy is on the same path..."

"You lied to me!" her son said, his voice bellowing from betrayal.

Angela spoke fast, Abel somehow understanding it all. "Please, Angel! I know you can't help everyone, but he hasn't yet lost his way. He is still young. Give him the strength to resist the Devil! Bring God to his heart!"

"I don't 'bring' anything," Abel replied in crude Tagalog. "I take away."

"Then take away his anger! It blinds him! It clouds his mind!"

"Fuck all of this!" Roberto yelled. He turned to leave, but Abel quickly grabbed his hand. Roberto cursed, tried to break free. Abel gripped him firmly. "Get the fuck off me!" the young man screamed.

Carlos rushed in and muscled Roberto in a bear hug, easily restraining him. Abel changed his hand-hold until *the feeling* returned. Roberto stopped struggling, a pointless effort with Carlos holding him. Once again, Abel felt a heavy weight pressed on him. He knelt to the carpet, still clutching the young man's hand.

"I ain't praying wit' you!" Roberto said, screaming.

"Ain't no one praying!" Abel said as he winced in pain, gripping Roberto's hand tighter. Carlos slowly freed the young man as he no longer offered resistance.

A moment later, Abel and Roberto released each other. To Roberto's shock, his rage and hate were gone, drifted away like a faded dream. The world was still imperfect, but no longer out to get him. Cops and teachers and social workers still didn't understand him, but were no longer his enemies. The system remained often unfair, but not bent to personally hold him down. His father and friends in prison weren't victims. They made many poor choices, hurt many people, all of which led to their interrupted lives.

Nothing changed yet everything did.

Everything seemed clear.

"Nanay?" Roberto turned to his mother, a single tear falling down his face. No one else mattered in that moment. He trembled, not sure what just happened. "I don't... I mean... Nay...?"

Angela threw her arms around her son as his mind now flooded with new thoughts, a new perspective, sympathy for his mother's ordeal.

"I'm sorry, Nay. I'm so sorry!"

Mother and son cried together for the first time since he was a boy. Carlos returned to the doorway, clearly touched by the exchange but trying desperately to hide it. Abel's stone face betrayed a slight smile.

Angela looked at Abel. She could barely get her words out. "Thank you, my angel," she said in Tagalog.

"Remember," Abel said, "tell no one what happened here, or the darkness I took away may return."

Angela nodded as she reached into her purse. "I know you do not accept money, only what is made by my hands. I hope you will take this." She offered Abel a red rose wrapped around a crucifix. He hesitated, but accepted the kind gesture. "The rose is from my yard," she said. "The cross will help you with your work."

"Sure it will," Abel said in a cold, almost heartless tone.

Angela and Roberto held hands as they walked out of the motel room. Carlos followed but once again paused at the door, turning to his boss with a look of curiosity.

"Maybe one day you'll tell me what exactly happens when you hold a man's hand," Carlos said.

"One day."

"Yeah, and maybe you'll tell me how the hell you could talk to that woman? Since when do you know Filipino?"

"I know what I need to know," Abel said. "It's part of 'the gift,' if that's what we're calling it now."

Carlos nodded, considering his boss's cryptic words. He followed mother and son out of the room, shutting the door as they left.

Finally alone, Abel uncovered a shoebox on the bedside table, already filled with miniature bibles, crosses, candles, rosary beads, and pictures of the Virgin Mary.

He carelessly tossed Angela's crucifix into the shoebox.

Carlos once again sat at his office window, headphones on, magazine in hand. The roaring engine of a Dodge Viper ripped him out of his heavy metal trance as it parked in front of him, next to his lowrider. The driver stepped out, removed his sunglasses, and checked the address on a crumbled note from his coat pocket.

Mr. Brennan, a fifty-year-old white man in a disheveled suit, slammed the door of his Viper. His companion, Mr. Felix, a young Mexican man with a sour face, shirt and tie, joined him. Brennan stumbled up to the office and banged on the window, grabbing Carlos' attention.

Brennan looked around the old motel for a moment. He spoke with a watery, chain-smoker voice. "Damn, is this place even open for business? Looks condemned!"

"You two boys need a room?" Carlos grinned.

"I need more than that, tough guy." Brennan lifted his dress shirt, exposing his stomach. The sight shocked Carlos.

"Come with me," Carlos said, stepping out of his office.

In Room 23, Abel lit a new cigarette while gazing at a photo in his hand. His younger, tuxedo-clad self danced with a Black woman who blessed a flowing white gown. They twirled at a lavish party on a pier. From the photo, he could clearly hear the smooth jazz of that evening, the steady beat of the ocean waves, the wind over the water. He could smell the Chloé Eau de Parfum on the nape of her neck. Her scent pulled him back to that moment, made him feel as if he were floating off his feet.

A knock on the door halted the music, ripping him from that pier so long ago.

Carlos entered with Mr. Brennan, who quickly spotted the cigarette.

"At last we meet," Mr. Brennan said. "Bum a smoke?" Abel gave him his newly lit cigarette. He promptly took a long drag. "I'm quitting again, which just means I don't buy 'em no more."

"My name is Abel Grant."

Abel offered a handshake, but Brennan didn't take it. Instead, he puffed his cigarette with a slightly drunken smile. His voice thundered, as if he owned the joint. "So this is the place?" Mr. Brennan said. "And you're the guy, right? I mean, THE guy?" Abel kept his hand out. Brennan laughed at this foolish bit of ceremony. He turned to his companion. "Keep an eye on the car, Mr. Felix. They'll strip it skin-and-bones in this shit hole."

Felix nodded and stepped outside. Carlos followed, shutting the door as they left.

Brennan let Abel keep his hand out for a moment before finally taking it. "Call me Brennan."

"Who told you about me, Mr. Brennan?"

"How does this work?" Brennan said, ignoring his host. "You shout some voodoo shit? Dance around? Sacrifice a chicken?"

Abel approached his guest, smelling something strong. "Whiskey?"

"Bourbon. Just a touch."

"Perhaps a touch too much," Abel said. "Maybe you should come back tomorrow with a clear head."

"Ain't never had the pleasure of a clear head, amigo," Brennan said. "And maybe... maybe there is no tomorrow. Not for me." His tipsy smile fell away.

Abel stared at the drunk man. He relented and gestured for him to sit on the bed. "Tell me."

"How about I show you?"

Brennan lifted his shirt again, revealing his torso, every inch peppered with large discolored tumors. Abel was aghast, the sight morbid and shocking, though he kept his stone face.

"How long?" Abel asked.

"Years and years, in and out of hospitals, filling doctors' pockets while they spun their wheels. Years and years until I resort to fuckin' voodoo, rumors of a Black miracle worker in a broke down motel."

"You realize I may be unable to help you?"

Brennan tossed a thick roll of cash onto the bed. Abel didn't touch it, didn't even acknowledge it.

"Yeah, yeah," Mr. Brennan said. "I heard you do this shit pro bono. But in my experience, cold hard cash motivates everyone to work harder. Even super secret colored angels."

Carlos returned, witnessing the rare sight of his boss taken unaware. Abel stood near Brennan and took his hand. As before, he changed his grip several times, waiting for *the feeling* to come.

Mr. Brennan sat silently. For a moment he was a believer, hoping for a miracle. He was surprised, broken-hearted, when Abel released him and backed away.

"Mr. Brennan," Abel said. "I'm sorry, but you're beyond my help."

"Try again."

Abel nodded to Carlos to open the door.

"Try. Again."

Abel remained unmoved. Brennan's confidence and attitude disappeared as he reduced to a stuttering, desperate man. "This is... bullshit! The stories I heard... you helped far worse!"

"It doesn't matter how bad it is," Abel said. "What matters is how long you've lived with it."

"You wanted to know how I found out about you? Perez. Fuckin' Rodrigo Perez."

Brennan gave Abel a moment to remember Rodrigo. Abel nodded that, yes, he knew that name. He remembered every one of the hundreds of souls he helped over his nine years as a divine servant.

"Now, you're going to tell me," Abel said in a commanding tone. There'd be nothing further until he heard the full story.

Mr. Brennan threw his hands up as he recalled Rodrigo's story.

"I own warehouses in St. Nelia, next to the church. Perez loaded trucks. Brought a box of sweet bread every morning. Nice guy. That was before a forklift clipped him. Goddamn, there was so much blood. His legs were... Doctor said he'd limp for the rest of his life. And man, what a limp." Brennan pulled himself together, buttoning his shirt. "I could've let him go, but I felt for him. You see, I take care of my men. Then one day he comes in brand new. Smiling. Dancing a jig. Word was he had Jesse Owens's fuckin' legs now. So I asked him about it. He said he just prayed and healed. Not a peep about you."

Brennan gestured for another cigarette. Abel complied, lighting a new one for him. Brennan took another slow drag.

"I got churchy on Rodrigo," Mr. Brennan said, continuing. "I said that God told me to talk to him, all that bullshit. He finally said 'The Angel' healed him, but he wasn't allowed to tell me who."

"He didn't tell you, did he?"

"Nope. Even after I threatened to deport his ass. So I poked around. Goddamn son, you have touched a lot of fuckin' people around here. And they all say the same thing, that an Angel of God held their hand."

"They're wrong," Abel said. "God left long ago."

Brennan's emotions spiraled as he pulled a gun from his coat, holding it at his side. Abel and Carlos froze. Brennan's trembling voice rose.

"Why them?" Mr. Brennan demanded. "Old women with a foot in the grave? Junkie whores? Homeless pricks without a pot to piss in? You heal street trash but not me?"

Abel remained calm. Carlos stood ready at the door.

"There were many others beyond my help," Abel said, facing the desperate man with a look of apology.

Mr. Brennan's whimpering took a sharp turn. He suddenly screamed through tears. "You're a sadist! You prey on the superstition of these ignorant fools! Make them believe in you. But your little show, you don't do it for money, you do it for kicks! What kind of sick, twisted fuck are you?"

Brennan stormed at Abel, pressing his gun barrel to the bridge of his nose. Abel looked past the gun and spoke calmly to its owner. "I'm not afraid of that gun, Mr. Brennan, so you can put it away. And maybe you're right and this is all a con. The people I save? Maybe they saved themselves. Maybe they had the strength all along. I'd like to think that. Maybe all they needed was to believe in a miracle." Abel nodded to Carlos to open the door. "And maybe you can find some salvation in that when you leave."

"When I leave," Mr. Brennan said with a weak laugh.

Brennan spun the gun on himself, holding it to his temple. Carlos rushed him, slapped the gun down...

BLAM!

Brennan screamed in pain. In the struggle, he shot himself in his side, the bullet breaking through two ribs before embedding in his pancreas. He clutched his wound as blood streamed out.

Upon hearing the gunshot, Mr. Felix ran in. Carlos stopped him as Abel quickly pressed on Brennan's wound with both hands. Instantly, Abel felt the searing pain of the critical wound surge into him.

Carlos picked up Brennan's gun and tucked it in his back pocket. Abel held Brennan tight and close as the injured man continued to struggle and reel from shock. They collapsed to the floor, Abel never letting go. Carlos knelt and wrapped his massive arms around the flailing man, trying to keep him still.

After a tense struggle, Abel finally found *the feeling*.

Carlos got the feeling as well. After serving his boss for nine years, nearly a decade of devoted faith, trusting that the angel's gift was real and not merely a clever mentalist's trick, Carlos finally got his long-time wish. Entangled with Abel and Brennan on the floor, he became part of the moment.

For the first time, Carlos saw the full experience...

The room fell silent, as did the bustling barrio that surrounded the motel. Time slowed to a crawl, with a cowering Mr. Brennan and a disoriented Mr. Felix nearly frozen in place. The blood from Brennan's ribs ran pitch black, dripping like tar, pushing its way down his pant legs, landing onto the carpet with a loud, echoing boom.

Carlos felt as if he were kneeling in dense snow, his arms and legs impossibly cold and heavy, his knees fused to the floor. He saw the colors of the room drain away as everything became a blur, the sounds of his breath and heartbeat pounding and repeating like a bass drum in a grand hall.

Only Abel was in vivid color, his face in focus, as he moved freely within the creeping storm. It crowned his head with an aura of bright light, shining from behind, expanding, casting him in silhouette as the ominous glow overtook the room. Though Carlos feared being blinded by the sight, he dared not close his eyes as he took in the spectacle.

Abel released Mr. Brennan.

Instantly, the room and the rest of the world reverted to their normal state. Carlos rose to his feet, the jarring transition nearly knocking him over.

Abel placed his head on the corner of the bed. Exhausted, barely able to breathe, he draped his arms onto the mattress.

Mr. Brennan remained on his knees, enduring a strange sensation. Mr. Felix rushed to tend to his employer only to be waved away. Brennan pulled up his shirt to discover an alarming amount of blood without a wound, all traces of the gunshot vanished.

Abel crawled to the bathroom and bowed over the toilet. He spewed a rush of bloody vomit, filling the bowl completely red. He slowly climbed up the sink to stand. A bullet fell from his hand and plunked onto the tile floor. Abel washed himself with a gallon jug of water over the dead faucet, splashing it onto his face and shoulders, filling the sink with red water.

Mr. Brennan sat stunned speechless as he watched Abel. He realized that what just transpired in that old motel room was indeed a miracle. He knew that the man reeling at the sink, trying to regain himself, truly served a higher power, an audacious claim he'd been told for months. All those poor souls who regaled him with stories of the angel at the Royal Queen Motel spoke the truth, a truth that a man like Mr. Brennan never would have believed if he hadn't been touched by it.

Abel looked up from the sink and saw the realization and hope in Brennan's eyes. "Mr. Brennan," Abel said, struggling to catch his breath. "You're still going to die, just not today, not from that bullet."

Disappointed and dejected, Mr. Brennan had no words, but his earlier desperation had left him. He rose to his feet, straightened his blood-soaked shirt and coat, and wandered to the door.

Abel called to him. "Payment, Mr. Brennan."

Confused, Brennan turned to Abel, looked at the men staring speechless at him. He spied the roll of cash still sitting unwanted on the bed. He considered it for a moment before picking it up and pocketing it. He offered Abel his wristwatch. "The only real Rolex in this part of town. We good?"

"Something you made."

Mr. Brennan thought for a moment. He pulled his wallet from his coat and removed a business card from it. He offered both the watch and the card. "The only thing I ever made is my business. I built it from nothing, brick by brick."

Abel reluctantly accepted the payment. He looked at the card: "Brennan Storage and Transport."

"Call me if you need anything," Mr. Brennan said. "Anything. Everyone in this neighborhood needs me, eventually. It's the one thing you and I have in common." He looked to Carlos, who still held his gun in his back pocket. Mr. Felix held his own gun at his side, waiting for his boss's next word.

"You can keep that, too," Brennan said, eyeing his old gun. "I don't need it no more." He nodded to his companion. Mr. Felix opened the door and the two men stepped outside.

Rather than follow them, Carlos promptly shut the door, remaining with his boss. He peered through the window blinds to watch them drive away.

Abel collapsed onto the bed and stared at the cracked ceiling. "You still want to know what happens when I hold a man's hand? You still need to know if it's all real? How it came to be? It started with my wife... my queen... nine years ago, may her soul eventually rest in peace."

Carlos had no ready response. He wanted to learn everything Abel would offer but hadn't the strength to listen.

"One day, Boss," he said, the words drifting out.

He opened the door and gazed out at the decaying barrio, at the empty parking lot baking in the sun that would soon have more grief-stricken visitors who heard about the angel at the old, abandoned motel on the edge of the St. Nelia District.

Carlos left Abel alone in the room.

Abel looked at Brennan's Rolex, nearly forgetting it was in his hand. He admired the gaudy trinket for a moment before tossing it carelessly into the shoebox.

Lionheart Park Retirement Village offers its residents a luxurious resort setting with quaint cottages by the sea. Within this paradise is a profound sorrow, a need to feel loved again. Eloise spends her time in the garden caring for the flowers and statues. Her lonely routine takes a turn when she finds a wounded crow that changes everyone's lives.

Family can be found in the unlikeliest of places in this novella by veteran writer Lynn Harrod.

Keepers of the Night Garden
Available on
www.deerwoodpress.com

About the Author

Lynn Harrod is an award-winning writer, artist, filmmaker, and educator with over 30 years of experience crafting short stories, essays, and screenplays. His characters often find their worlds spun sideways by a startling revelation.

Lynn was awarded the PRSA Image Award of Excellence and has placed in the Quarterfinals and Semifinals of the Nicholl Fellowship, the Finals of the Nevada Film Office Competition, the Semifinals of the Writers' Network Competition, and twice in the Semifinals of the FadeIn Awards.

Born in Texas, raised in California's San Joaquin Valley, and educated and trained in Hollywood, Lynn is a writer and partner with Only Human Productions, where several of his works are in development. When he's not spending time with his wife and daughter, or writing all night on his patio, he's usually having a pint with friends.